TUMTUM AND NUTMEG:
THE PIRATES' TREASURE

TUMTUM AND NUTMEG: THE PIRATES' TREASURE

Emily Bearn

Illustrated by Nick Price

First published 2009
by Egmont UK Limited
This Large Print edition published by
AudioGO Ltd
by arrangement with
Egmont Books 2011

ISBN: 978 1405 664592

British Library Cataloguing in Publication Data

Printed and bound in Great Britain by
CPI Antony Rowe, Chippenham and Eastbourne

For my mother

CHAPTER ONE

It was a fine May morning, with not a scent of trouble in the air. The sort of morning, as Tumtum noted happily, that bore the promise of a very uneventful day. He rose from his bed, and set off for the kitchen—and the kitchen was a long way from the bedroom, for Nutmouse Hall was a big house, with long corridors and lots of stairs.

As he went, he remembered all the things he had to do. There was breakfast, elevenses, lunch, tea and supper to eat, and a newspaper to read, and a nap to fit in. And that is a lot of events in a day which promises to be uneventful.

Tumtum pressed on, keen to get started. But when he reached the kitchen he found Nutmeg in a terrible fuss.

'Something dreadful's happened!' she cried.

'What, dear?' Tumtum asked, sitting down at the table. Nutmeg often fussed, and usually about the silliest things—such as an upset vase, or a broken mug.

Even so, it struck Tumtum that this morning she looked more flustered than usual.

'It's the children,' she said miserably.

'Why? Is one of them ill?' Tumtum replied.

'Oh, no. Nothing like that. Something much worse.'

'Gracious. Have they died?' Tumtum said, looking shocked.

'Oh, no, no. Not that. But something almost—well, something terrible, all the same.' She sat down and looked at him very solemnly. 'Arthur and Lucy are going to spend the night outdoors. *In a tent.*'

Tumtum looked relieved. Dear Nutmeg! It was just like her to make a fuss and bother about nothing. He took the lid off the serving dish, and helped himself to some scrambled eggs. 'Why are you so concerned? I'm sure they'll have a lovely time,' he said.

'But think about all the things that could go wrong,' Nutmeg wailed. 'I heard them planning everything just now, when I went to borrow some butter from the kitchen, and I'm sure it will end in

2

disaster. They're using an old tent which Arthur found in the garden shed. Well I wouldn't be surprised if it leaks—'

'If it rains they can come back inside,' Tumtum interrupted. 'Their father is sure to leave the kitchen door unlocked for them. Now don't look so anxious, dear. I don't see how they could come to any harm camping out in the garden on a warm summer's night. Besides, we'll be able to creep outside and check on them.'

'No we won't,' Nutmeg groaned. 'That's the whole point. Oh, don't you see, Tumtum? The children have no intention of sleeping in the garden. They're going to camp by the stream!'

'Are you sure?' Tumtum asked. Now he looked anxious too. The stream ran along the bottom of the meadow behind Rose Cottage. It was at least a quarter of a mile from the house, and quarter of a mile would seem a very long way if you were a mouse.

'I am quite sure,' Nutmeg said. 'I heard the whole conversation. At first they were going to pitch the tent in the garden, then Arthur suggested they go down to the stream. And of course Lucy went along with it, because she thinks it will be more of an adventure. And now they seem to think they're going on a real safari. They want to light a campfire, and fry sausages on it, and boil a kettle to make tea!'

'Don't they have to be at school tomorrow?' Tumtum asked.

'No. They're on half-term. They don't have to be back at school until Monday.'

'Hmmm,' said Tumtum. 'What does their father say about it?'

'Oh, you know what Mr Mildew's like. He wouldn't notice if they stayed away for a month.'

Tumtum looked thoughtful. It was true that Mr Mildew was very absent-minded. He was an inventor by trade, and he spent all day long shut away in his study, inventing silly things such as grape-peelers and singing key rings. He had little interest in anything other than his work. As often as not he wouldn't even notice what time of day it was, and then he would get all his meals muddled up, and give Arthur and Lucy tinned spaghetti for breakfast, and porridge for tea.

Nutmeg was right. He would be too absorbed in his latest invention to worry about what his children were up to.

'When do they plan to set off?' Tumtum asked.

'This afternoon, about teatime,' Nutmeg replied. 'They're going to spend the morning packing.'

'Well, if they've made up their minds, then I can't think how we can stop them,' Tumtum said. 'We shall just have to hope for the best. I can't see that much will go wrong. Lucy's very responsible and—'

'Hope for the best?' Nutmeg cried. 'I will have you know, Mr Nutmouse, that I am not going to watch those children set off all alone across that vast meadow, and then just sit here as though nothing has happened, *hoping for the best.*'

Tumtum was taken aback. Nutmeg only called him 'Mr Nutmouse' when she was very, very cross. 'Then what do you propose we do?' he asked feebly.

'Nutmeg started picking at the tea-cosy, avoiding Tumtum's eyes. He could sense she was about to say something he wouldn't like. When she looked up, her expression was very fierce. 'There's only one thing for it,' she said. 'If Arthur and Lucy are going camping, then we're going too.'

CHAPTER TWO

'But, my dear. You don't propose we sleep *outdoors*?' Tumtum asked nervously. He had lived all his life in Nutmouse Hall, which was an unusually grand house, with tapestries, and paintings, and a ballroom, and a billiards room, and a banqueting room—and just about every other sort of room a mouse might want. So the thought of sleeping outdoors was very strange to him. At home he always slept in a four-poster bed.

'That is exactly what I propose,' Nutmeg replied. 'We'll follow the children to the stream and set up camp alongside them. Then at the very least we shall be on hand should any trouble arise.'

'But we haven't got a tent,' Tumtum protested.

'Yes we have. General Marchmouse gave us one as a wedding present—don't you remember, dear? And it comes with two inflatable mattresses, so we shall be quite comfortable.'

Tumtum groaned. He had forgotten all about the General's present, for their wedding had been a long while ago. He had thought it a silly present at the time, for why would he want a tent when he had a house with seventeen bedrooms? He had never been camping before, and he felt sure he wouldn't like it.

'Now,' Nutmeg said impatiently, 'hurry up and finish your eggs, we've a lot to do.'

As soon as the breakfast had been cleared away, the Nutmouses sat down at the kitchen table and made a list of all the things they would need for their expedition.

'Let's see,' Nutmeg said, nibbling the end of her pencil thoughtfully. 'I shall make sausage rolls and centipede pasties, and a pâté and a soup—dandelion, I think—and a walnut loaf and a ginger cake, and an apple tart and a strawberry trifle. And we shall need a bottle of wine and a frying pan, and a kettle and the picnic china, and two forks and four knives and six spoons . . . oh, and bless me if I'm not forgetting the napkins, and the salt cellar, and the

9

pepper grinder, and the folding chairs and—'

'Steady on, dear. We shall only be away one night,' Tumtum said.

'Yes, but we shall be gone for tea and supper and breakfast—and as likely as not for elevenses as well,' Nutmeg replied, adding a further item to her list.

'Tea and supper and breakfast—and as likely as not elevenses as well,' Tumtum said thoughtfully. 'That's a lot of food. And there's the camping equipment too. How will we carry everything across the meadow?'

Nutmeg frowned. Tumtum was right, they would never manage it all. But then she had an idea. 'The children will have to carry us,' she said. 'We can hide inside one of their rucksacks before they set off, and hitch a lift. I shouldn't think they'll notice a few extra ounces.'

'It will be more than a few ounces,' Tumtum grumbled. But he had nothing better to suggest.

So when Nutmeg's list was completed, they started to get everything ready. Tumtum busied himself in the butler's pantry, filling a wicker basket with

10

crockery, while Nutmeg bustled about in the kitchen, making delicious things to eat.

'If we must go camping, then we might as well do it properly,' Tumtum muttered as he polished the wine glasses.

*   *   *

It was gone lunchtime before the Nutmouses were ready.

'We had better get aboard the rucksacks, or the children might leave without us,' Nutmeg said.

'But it's only two o'clock,' Tumtum replied. 'You said they weren't going to leave until teatime.'

'Yes, but you know what humans are like. Teatime could mean anything. Now come on. We can't risk being left behind.'

Tumtum could see there was no point arguing. So he helped Nutmeg drag everything through to the hall, then they staggered out of their front door. Tumtum was bent double, hauling the tent, the picnic table, the two folding chairs and a mass of plates and

11

silverware. Nutmeg followed behind, heaving the hamper and the cooking pots.

Tumtum locked the door behind him, then they trudged across the broom cupboard floor, and through the little iron gates covering their mouse-hole. On the other side of the gates lay the Mildews' kitchen.

None of the Mildews knew they had a broom cupboard behind their kitchen wall, because there had always been a big Welsh dresser hiding the cupboard door from view. The Nutmouses' front gates were behind the dresser, and they always came and went very quietly, so as not to give their hiding place away. It would be a terrible thing if the Mildews were to discover the broom cupboard door.

So that afternoon the mice closed the gates very quietly, and did not make so much as a squeak as they crept out into the dark, dusty patch beneath the dresser.

'Wait here. I'll check there's no one about,' Tumtum whispered. Then he went to the edge of the dresser and poked his nose into the kitchen.

The room was empty, but he could hear the children talking outside in the hallway. And he could see their rucksacks lying beside the garden door. They were already packed very full. One rucksack even had a frying pan poking out at the top.

On the floor beside them was Arthur's wooden boat—a pretty blue yacht, about the size of a man's shoe, with white sails and the name *Bluebottle* written on the stern. Tumtum had seen the boat before. It lived in the attic of Rose Cottage. And now he supposed Arthur intended to sail it on the stream.

He suddenly imagined the boat racing through the icy water, crashing over the pebbles, and he felt himself shiver. Tumtum had never been sailing before, and the very thought of it filled him with fear. He was glad that he and Nutmeg would be staying on dry land.

He took one more look round the kitchen, standing very still and listening to the silence. He felt uneasy. He and Nutmeg usually visited Rose Cottage at night, when the Mildews were asleep. It felt reckless to venture out in daylight, when there was such a risk of being seen.

'Come on,' he whispered to Nutmeg. 'The rucksacks are by the door. We can get in now, while there's no one here.'

The Nutmouses lugged their things across the kitchen, beneath the towering table and chairs. But just as they were reaching the far side of the room, the floor gave a sudden tremor, and Arthur and Lucy walked in.

The mice froze. They were standing at the base of the first rucksack, which rose above them like a hill. In order to wriggle inside they would have to climb to the very top—and if they did that, Arthur and Lucy would be sure to see them.

The children were standing by the table. They might look round at any moment.

'What shall we do?' Nutmeg trembled. She was so frightened she could feel her heart going thump.

They stood there helplessly, wishing the kitchen tiles would swallow them. Then Tumtum noticed a bulging pocket on the side of the rucksack, just a few centimetres above their heads.

'Look, we can hide in there!' he said. 'You go first, and I'll hand everything up to you.'

He hoisted Nutmeg on to the base of the rucksack, then she pulled herself up by a buckle, and crawled into the pocket under the flap.

A moment later her head peeked out, her face full of anxiety. 'Hurry, dear!' she urged, as Tumtum started passing her all their clobber. There seemed no end to it. First came the picnic hamper, then the table, then the two folding chairs . . . Nutmeg snatched each item hurriedly, terrified that the children might look their way.

'That's everything,' Tumtum panted, as he handed her the basket of crockery. Then he scrambled up the buckle and wriggled into the pocket beside her.

There followed a long wait. The Nutmouses could hear the children coming and going in the kitchen, but they seemed in no hurry to set off. The pocket was pitch black, and very stuffy. But the mice dared not lift the flap for fear of being seen.

They sat side by side on the hamper,

15

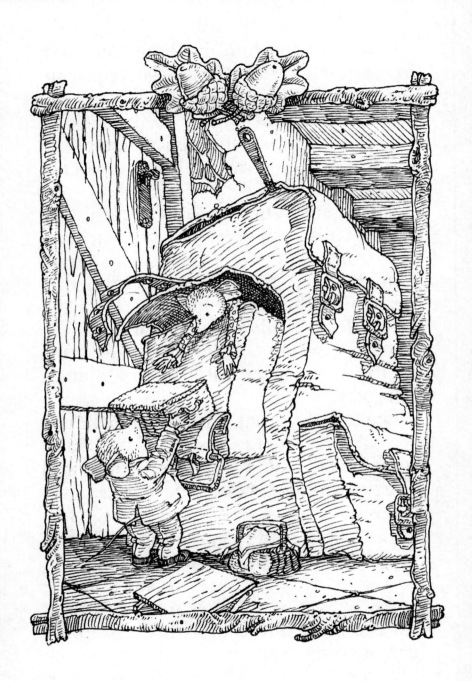

16

nervously nibbling a sausage roll. An hour or more slipped by. They started to wonder if the children had decided not to go camping after all.

'Surely there couldn't be any harm in poking my nose out, just for a second?' Nutmeg suggested restlessly.

'No, dear. It's too dangerous,' Tumtum replied—and even as he spoke, the children's voices got nearer. Next thing, the Nutmouses felt themselves soaring into the air as Arthur hoisted the rucksack on to his shoulder.

They could not see out, and yet there were some clues as to where they were going. They heard the back door being slammed behind them, as the children went outside. And then they heard the garden gate opening and shutting, and they knew they had entered the meadow.

'Let's go this way,' Lucy said. Then she and Arthur started walking downhill, towards the stream.

*   *   *

It was horribly bumpy in the rucksack pocket, and Nutmeg soon began to feel

17

sick. But the children hadn't far to go—at least, not by human standards. And in what seemed like no time Lucy said, 'Let's camp here'; and suddenly the rucksack fell to the ground with a crash.

'I think we've landed,' Tumtum said, feeling very bruised. He slowly picked himself up, and peeked outside. 'We're beside the stream, next to the old oak tree,' he reported. 'Come on, let's get out of here before the children find us.'

While Arthur and Lucy were unpacking their tent, the mice threw all their things out of the pocket, then clambered down to the ground. They felt safer now, for the grass was much taller than they were. They would be well hidden.

'Where shall we set up camp?' Nutmeg said.

'How about just over there, under that clump of nettles?' Tumtum suggested. 'So long as we're under stinging nettles, the children won't trample on us. But we'll still be close enough to keep an eye on them.'

'Good idea,' Nutmeg agreed. 'And we can light our campfire behind that

pebble. We shall be completely hidden.'

So the Nutmouses carried everything through the long grass, and started setting up camp.

Although Tumtum hesitated to admit it, everything was very luxurious. The General's tent was well proportioned— bigger than the butler's pantry at Nutmouse Hall, and tall enough to stand up in—so the Nutmouses did not have to squeeze together, as some campers do.

Tumtum blew up the inflatable mattresses, and Nutmeg made up their beds with feather sleeping bags and soft pillows. Then they unfolded the picnic table, and laid it with plates and glasses and silver candlesticks, and damask table-napkins embroidered with the Nutmouse family crest. And after that, Tumtum made a big fire out of twigs, while Nutmeg marinated some earwigs for dinner.

It was the most magnificent display of camping you have ever seen. But the children's campsite was another story.

CHAPTER THREE

Everything was going wrong for Arthur and Lucy.

They had managed to erect their tent, but it looked much smaller than the one shown in the instructions. And it was sagging in the middle.

'We can't both fit in *that*,' Lucy said, feeling very disappointed.

Arthur shrugged. 'You can sleep in it. I'll sleep on the grass. It's the campfire I'm worried about. You are a dolt, Lucy, forgetting to bring the matches.'

'Oh, don't start that again. It wasn't me who was meant to remember them— they were on your list.'

'No they weren't.'

Lucy was about to say, 'Yes they were,' but she thought better of it, because then there would have been a row, and everything really would have been spoiled.

'There's no point bickering about it,' she said. 'But whatever happens I'm not going back to the house to get them. If

Pa sees us he might not let us out again.'

Their father had seemed disapproving when they had asked if they could go camping for the night. And at one stage they thought he might not let them. But he had agreed to it in the end, and they suspected that by now he had probably forgotten they'd gone. But if they went back to the cottage to look for matches, it might start the whole thing up again.

'We'll just have to make do without a fire,' Lucy said. 'It's very warm, it's not as though we need one.'

'But how will we cook supper?' Arthur asked. He had been looking forward to cooking supper all day. They had brought pots and pans, and sausages and eggs and sunflower oil, and even a tin of macaroni cheese.

'We'll have to eat the macaroni cheese cold. And we can have the tinned peaches for pudding,' Lucy said practically.

Arthur made a face, imagining what cold macaroni cheese would taste like. But then there was another disaster.

'Where's the tin-opener?' Lucy asked, emptying both rucksacks on to the grass. 'Don't say you've forgotten that as well.'

'I thought you packed it,' Arthur said.

'Well I thought you packed it,' Lucy replied testily. 'But since neither of us packed it, I suppose we'll have to go home. If we can't open the tins, then there really is nothing to eat—unless you like raw sausages.'

'You can go home if you like, but I'm staying here,' Arthur said. He was determined to spend a night outdoors, even if it meant he had to starve. He looked very stubborn.

'Oh, all right, I'll stay too,' she said unhappily, for she felt it wouldn't be right to leave him on his own. 'But this is the last time I'm going camping with you—ever!'

*   *   *

The Nutmouses sipped their dandelion soup, observing this unhappy scene.

Nutmeg would willingly have given the children her own supper, but it would have been much too small. They could have eaten the Nutmouses' entire hamper in one bite.

'Couldn't we at least get their campfire

23

going, dear?' she asked. The children had gathered a big pile of wood from under the trees along the stream. It seemed a terrible shame that it couldn't be lit.

'It's too big. Our matches could never light branches that size,' Tumtum said. And he was right, of course, for each of their matches was smaller than an ant.

'But we must do *something*,' Nutmeg went on. 'We can't just sit here and watch them go without supper.'

'Certainly not,' agreed Tumtum, who never missed a meal. But he could see this problem was not going to be easily solved. 'Let's have a sautéed earwig,' he suggested, for sautéed earwigs always helped him think more clearly.

'All right, dear. I'll clear the soup bowls,' Nutmeg said. But as she stood up they heard a sudden bang. The children didn't hear it, for it was too quiet for human ears. But it gave the Nutmouses a tremendous fright. It sounded like a gun going off.

Nutmeg clung to her chair. Her face had gone very pale.

'It's probably just a field mouse out

hunting,' Tumtum said, trying to reassure her. But she could hear the fear in his voice too. Tumtum stood up and peered warily into the grass, unsure which direction the noise had come from. Then he heard something rustling towards them. Nutmeg heard it too, and gave a shriek—then all at once a creature sprang out in front of them and shouted 'BOO!'

The Nutmouses both jumped. But they were very relieved when they saw who it was.

'General Marchmouse!' Tumtum exclaimed. 'Gracious, what a fright you gave us!'

'That was my intention,' the General chuckled. 'I spotted you through my field glasses, having a quiet little dinner out of doors, so I decided to jolly things up. "Ha, ha!" I thought. "I shall let off my gun, then creep up through the grass, and pounce on them shouting, 'BOO!' That'll make 'em jump!"'

Nutmeg looked disapproving. She thought it a very silly prank. 'What are you doing out so late?' she asked.

'I am beetle hunting,' the General

replied, patting his rifle. 'I've been out since dawn but it's been a rotten day. I haven't shot a single bug. Anyway,' he continued, sitting down on Tumtum's chair and helping himself to some soup, 'what are you two doing here, more to the point? Babysitting, from the look of things.'

'That's right,' Nutmeg said. ' We came to keep an eye on the children. We heard them planning a camping trip, and we didn't want to let them go out alone. But I'm afraid we haven't been much help. They need matches and a tin-opener, but we can't give them ours as they are much too small.'

The General stood up, and studied the children's camp through his field glasses. 'What a poor show,' he said disapprovingly.

'They're not usually like this,' Nutmeg replied defensively. 'It's just that they forgot—'

'Leave this to me,' the General interrupted. 'I'll soon have things shipshape.' He took his rifle from his shoulder, and stuffed it full of bullets. Then he marched purposefully towards

the children's tent.

The Nutmouses watched in terror, wondering what he would do. Arthur and Lucy were playing by the stream, so the General was able to approach unseen. He made first for the tin of peaches, which was standing upright in the grass, beside Arthur's rucksack, and aimed his gun straight at it. The General had a seasoned eye and with an immaculate volley of fire, he blasted the top right off.

Tumtum and Nutmeg pressed their paws over their ears, for the gun made a dreadful din. The first round was quickly followed by a second, as the General blew open the tin of macaroni cheese.

Nutmeg shrieked. But there was more to come. The General reached a hand to his belt, and unclipped a grenade. (General Marchmouse always carried a grenade when he went outdoors, on the basis that you never knew when a grenadish situation might occur.)

He removed the pin, and took aim. Then he bowled the grenade full tilt into the children's campfire. And no sooner had he let it go than he raced for cover, throwing himself flat on the ground behind a tent-peg. The grenade was no bigger than a raisin, but it went off with a huge bang—enough to make the Nutmouses' tent wobble. Then there was a brilliant burst of light as the campfire exploded into flames.

When the General finally sauntered back to the dinner table, he was looking understandably pleased with himself.

CHAPTER FOUR

The children were beside the stream, and did not hear the General's grenade going off. But when they looked round a few moments later, they saw the flames dancing from the campfire. They were astonished, for fires don't light themselves. They had only been away from the camp for a few minutes, and they could see all the way across the meadow, so they were sure they would have spotted someone coming.

'Come on,' Arthur said, running back to the tent. 'Let's look in the grass. If anyone's been here they'll have left tracks.' But though they searched all round the camp, they could find only the tracks they had made themselves, going back and forth to the stream.

Lucy was frightened, for it was odd to think of someone creeping up and lighting the fire, then vanishing without trace. But she had an even bigger surprise when she noticed that the tins had been opened.

'That's really spooky,' Arthur said, examining them very carefully. 'They haven't been opened with a tin-opener.'

'Then how have they been opened?' Lucy asked nervously. She could feel herself shiver. It was not yet dark, but the meadow had become eerie. She felt a sudden urge to run back to the cottage— and yet somehow her legs wouldn't carry her. But then Arthur said something which made everything much better.

'It must have been Nutmeg.'

Lucy felt her breath come back again. Of course it was her! For who else could it have been? She must have followed them from the cottage, and when she saw that they couldn't light the fire and that they didn't have a tin-opener she must have crept up and put everything right.

'It would be just like her,' Arthur said.

'But how could she have opened the tins?' Lucy asked. 'I mean—well, she's very small, isn't she?'

The children had never set eyes on Nutmeg, and they did not know that she was a mouse. In her letters to them, she had called herself a fairy, so that's what they thought she was. And they knew how tiny she must be, for they had found a pair of her slippers in the doll's house, and each was no bigger than a ladybird.

'Oh, she'd have found a way,' Arthur replied confidently. 'Think of all the things she's done in Rose Cottage—sealing windows, and lighting boilers, and unblocking sinks. Opening a tin of macaroni cheese must have been easy compared to all that.'

'Where do you think she is now then?' Lucy asked.

'Oh, I don't know,' Arthur shrugged. 'I suppose she's hiding in the grass somewhere.'

'Goodness,' Lucy said. 'And there we were, thinking it must have been a ghost or something.'

'*You* might have thought so, but I don't believe in ghosts,' Arthur said grandly.

'Oh, all right, I know,' Lucy replied. She was feeling much too relieved to argue about who believed in what. 'Come on, now the fire's lit we might as well have supper. I'm starving.'

The two children hurriedly set about preparing their food, for they had eaten

nothing since lunch. But supper did not take long to cook. They poked the fire with a stick, making a flat patch to cook on. Then they fried the sausages and eggs in oil, and heated the macaroni cheese in a saucepan. Everything got a bit burned. But when you are sitting by a campfire watching the sun sink over a meadow, even burned food doesn't taste too bad.

As night gathered, the stream started to fill with black shadows. But when they looked back across the meadow the children could still see the familiar sight of Rose Cottage, silhouetted against the darkening sky. Presently a dim gleam appeared in the downstairs window, as their father turned on the kitchen light. Suddenly Lucy wished she was back in her comfortable attic bed.

'Let's wash up in the morning. It's too dark now,' she said when they had finished supper. And Arthur agreed, for he had also noticed how black the stream had become. It would be much too frightening to wash up in it now.

'We might as well go to bed, seeing as it's getting dark,' he said.

'All right. But remember the tent's too small for two—you're sleeping on the grass,' Lucy said teasingly. Arthur's face fell. 'Oh, come on,' she laughed, 'we can both squeeze inside.'

*   *   *

The Nutmouses and the General, who were still finishing their enormous dinner, watched as Arthur and Lucy crawled into the tent. Arthur had turned his torch on and they could see the children illuminated through the canvas. It was clearly a terrible squish.

'Another slither, anyone?' Nutmeg asked, offering round the cheese board.

'Not for me, dear,' replied Tumtum, who had eaten the lion's share of the trifle, not to mention half the apple pie. 'I don't know about you, but I'm ready to turn in. All this fresh air has gone to my head. And hadn't you better be getting home, General? Mrs Marchmouse must be getting worried about you.'

'Oh, poppycock! Mrs Marchmouse knows better than to worry about me,' the General replied breezily. ' "If I'm not home by bedtime, just leave the door on the latch," I said. So you see, Nutmouse, I am a free mouse tonight! And I intend to camp out here, with you!'

Tumtum and Nutmeg looked taken aback. You have to be very fond of a mouse to let him share your tent. And fond as they were of General Marchmouse, they weren't as fond of him as all that.

'I'm afraid you would find it rather uncomfortable, General. Our tent is only equipped for two,' Tumtum said tactfully.

'Oh, fiddlesticks! I'm not going to sleep in that,' the General replied. He stood up, and pointed towards Arthur's toy boat, *Bluebottle*, which was standing beside the children's tent. 'I shall sleep in there!'

'Don't be a fool, General,' Tumtum said. 'Imagine if Arthur finds you on board. He might take you prisoner again!'

Not so long ago, the children had found the General exploring their doll's house, and there had been terrible consequences. For they had put him in a biscuit tin, then taken him to their school, and rehoused him in a cage full of pet gerbils. The children had thought the General would be happy there, but in fact he had been miserable. And if the Nutmouses hadn't rounded up a troupe of daredevil ballerinas to rescue him he would never have escaped.

You might have thought the General would have learned his lesson. But the sight of *Bluebottle* had thrown him. Unbeknown to the Nutmouses, he had been dreaming about her all through supper. In his mind's eye, he could see himself as *Bluebottle*'s Captain, coursing down the stream and harpooning salmon from the deck. That little blue boat had stirred a fierce longing in his heart. He *had* to spend the night on board.

'Do stop fussing, Nutmouse,' he said, slinging his kit bag on to his shoulder. 'I won't let Arthur find me. I just want somewhere to lay my head until dawn.'

Then the General was gone.

'Well if he wants to go, we can't stop him,' Nutmeg said as they watched him disappear through the grass. 'Anyway, I can't see he'll come to much harm if he sleeps on *Bluebottle* tonight. We'll just have to make sure he disembarks before the children wake up.'

'Hmmm. I suppose so,' Tumtum said. He couldn't face running after him now, for he was too tired for an argument. But the thought of the General strutting about on Arthur's boat made Tumtum very uneasy.

*   *   *

While the Nutmouses retired to their tent, General Marchmouse stole on board. He climbed up *Bluebottle*'s finely crafted rigging, and dropped down on to the moonlit deck, rubbing his paws with glee at the sight of the toy cannon, and the crow's-nest, and the shiny wooden steering wheel. It was a proper old-fashioned war vessel—and he was in command!

With a stirring heart, he took out his torch, and crept down the narrow stairs leading below deck. And here lay more delights—a storeroom full of plastic cannonballs, and a tin soldier, and a

39

40

master cabin, with a bed and a dressing table and a chest of drawers. Everything was mouse-sized.

The General sat down at the dressing table and preened his whiskers in the mirror, thinking what a handsome captain he would make. Then he closed his eyes, and started to dream. He fancied he could hear the spray lashing his cabin window, and the waves crashing on the deck. Oh, what adventures he could have, if only he were out on the open water, instead of being stuck here in the grass!

It was all very frustrating. But then an idea came to him. It was a simple idea, but none the worse for that. Instead of creeping out of the boat first thing in the morning, before the children woke up, he would simply stay on board.

Arthur will never notice me, so long as I keep below deck, he thought. *I'll hide under the bed while he carries the boat down to the stream. Then as soon as he's launched her in the water I shall rush upstairs, and tighten the sails, and grab the wheel, and sail away as fast as the flow will carry me. I shall take the ship. And phooey to anyone who tries to stop me!*

Delighted with his plan, the General stretched out on the Captain's bed, and drifted into a very deep sleep.

CHAPTER FIVE

Next morning the Nutmouses woke at dawn, as the light began to fill their tent. 'I'll bring you a cup of tea,' Tumtum yawned. Then he pulled on his dressing gown, and went outside to stoke the fire. It was a fine day, warm and cloudless, but there was a gentle breeze rustling the grass. There was no sound of voices coming from the children's tent—and not a squeak from the General.

'Is anyone else up?' Nutmeg asked when Tumtum returned with the tea-tray.

'Not yet,' he replied. 'Anyway, you know what the General's like. I remember when he was staying at Nutmouse Hall, he never got up before nine.'

'Oh, gracious,' Nutmeg said. 'I'd forgotten all about him. Well we can't let him stay on *Bluebottle* until nine. The children might find him.'

'I know. But we'll have a hard job waking him,' Tumtum said. 'He hates

43

getting out of bed.'

'Let's take him some breakfast, that should help to get him going.' Nutmeg suggested.

'All right, but we'd better hurry,' Tumtum replied. 'I know it's early, but there's still a risk that the children will wake up.'

They quickly got dressed, then Nutmeg fried some sausages while Tumtum prepared a thermos of coffee. When everything was ready, they packed it into the picnic hamper, and hastened towards the boat. There was a ladder dangling from the stern. They climbed up it, carrying the hamper between them, then scrambled over the railing on to the deck. The breeze was gathering, batting the sail, and as the mice made their way downstairs they could feel the boat wobble.

'Here he is!' Tumtum said, finding the General in the master cabin, stretched out luxuriously on his bed.

'Rise and shine, General!' Nutmeg said cheerily, placing the hamper on the table. 'If you stay in bed any longer, your sausages will get cold.'

45

'Leave me alone. I want to sleep,' the General grunted.

'Well you shall have to sleep elsewhere,' Tumtum said sternly. 'If you stay here the children will find you. Or worse still, they might not find you, and launch the boat on the stream with you still in it! And you wouldn't want that would you?'

The General opened one eye, and looked at him crossly. Of course this was exactly what he wanted, and it was awfully tiresome of Tumtum to interfere with his plans. He rolled over, and lay with his face to the wall, wishing they would go away.

But then it occurred to him that if he was going to steal the boat, it would be much more fun if the Nutmouses came too. *Now there's an idea*, he thought. *If I can keep them on board long enough, then we can all sail away together! What a jolly adventure that would be!*

He suspected the Nutmouses would not be keen on this plan. So he had to be very crafty. He turned over, and watched as Nutmeg hurriedly unpacked the hamper, and laid the table for breakfast.

She kept looking through the porthole, to check the children hadn't emerged from their tent.

'Come on, General. Come and have a sausage,' she said.

The General yawned, and stretched each leg in turn. Then he sat up, and rose from his bed as slowly as he could. 'A fine morning,' he drawled. Then he slouched across to the dressing table, and set about grooming his chin.

'Do come and eat, General!' Nutmeg said impatiently. But when he finally sat down at the table, he did not guzzle his food as he normally did. He ate very daintily, taking tiny mouthfuls, and chewing each one for ages.

So breakfast dragged on a long time.

'I have appointed myself Captain of this vessel,' the General announced importantly, raising another crumb to his lips. 'You can be my First Mate, Mr Nutmouse. And you, Mrs Nutmouse,' he added generously, 'can be in charge of catering.'

'Don't be so silly,' Tumtum said. 'This is Arthur's boat, and if we dilly-dally here much longer he'll find us. Now

47

come on, General. Gather your things and let's be off.'

'*Captain*,' the General corrected him. 'I am a Captain now!'

Tumtum sighed. This was all too silly. But then Nutmeg pointed to the porthole and let out a shriek:

'The children are up!'

The Nutmouses grabbed the hamper, and rushed for the door. 'Hurry, General!' Nutmeg pleaded. But the General just sat tight, and went on eating.

'I shall not abandon my ship. You run along if you must, but I am staying here, where I belong. And I don't care if Arthur sees me,' he said.

Tumtum and Nutmeg looked at him in astonishment. Could he not see what danger they were in?

'Don't be a fool, General,' Tumtum began—but it was too late, for when they next looked back through the porthole they could see Arthur's hand reaching towards the boat. Nutmeg let out a cry of terror; then suddenly the floor lurched beneath them, and *Bluebottle* soared into the air.

The Nutmouses clung to a table leg as Arthur tucked the boat under his arm and carried it to the stream. They could see brief flashes of the ground through the porthole. It looked a horribly long way down.

But the General showed no fear. He was elated. Everything was going just as he had planned. 'Hurrah! We shall take command of the ship, and race away downstream!' he shrieked.

Then all at once the boat started plummeting through the air. The mice braced themselves on the floor—and the next instant there was a violent smack as *Bluebottle* hit the water.

The stream was flowing fast. The boat surged forward, her mast tilting to starboard as she pulled away from the bank. Then she righted herself midstream, and raced away with the current.

'We're away!' the General cheered, rushing from the cabin. 'All hands on deck!'

'For goodness' sake, stay down here or the children will see you!' Tumtum shouted. But the General was already halfway up the stairs.

Tumtum stumbled to the porthole, and pressed his nose against the glass. He could see Arthur and Lucy chasing after them along the bank. But the stream was widening now, and *Bluebottle* had been swept out of their reach. He looked down at the rushing water, and felt a dread rising in his stomach. He staggered out of the cabin, and followed the General up to the deck. *Bluebottle* was going at a ferocious pace. There was spray cutting overhead, and the breeze was thrashing the sails.

'We must change course and steer back to the bank,' Tumtum shouted, clinging to the mast. 'For pity's sake, General! If we continue at this rate we shall be swept out to sea!'

'Hurrah!' cried the General, who could think of nothing nicer. He ran across the deck and grabbed the steering wheel. He twisted it left, then right, then left again, making the boat lurch violently. He had a mad look in his eyes.

'Faster! Faster!' he squealed, as the waves crashed upon the deck.

'You'll capsize us, you fool!' Tumtum

51

shouted. He made to grab the wheel, but the General clung on tight. Then followed the most desperate of scenes, in which Tumtum tried to wrestle the General to the ground—it was a real fisticuffs, with pummeling and slugging, and cries of 'Pow!' and 'Oof!' and 'Ouch!'

But just as they were getting into full swing, the boat suddenly slowed down, almost to a halt, and gave a deep shudder. The mice stopped fighting and stood up, wondering what had happened. To their surprise they saw that they had left the stream behind them. And now they were floating in a huge pool of still, clear water.

'Gracious,' Tumtum said. 'We're in The Pond.' There was awe in his voice, for The Pond was a wild place. It was bigger than a tennis court. And if, like Tumtum, you were only six centimetres tall, a tennis court would seem as big as an ocean.

When a mouse stood on The Pond's shore, he could not see to the other side. He could see only a long, blue horizon. As for what lay beyond the horizon, he could only guess, for no mouse had ever sailed across The Pond before. It looked so big, none had dared.

But General Marchmouse would change all that.

'The Pond!' he whispered breathlessly. 'I shall be the first mouse to explore it! I'll sail over the horizon, and conquer whatever lies beyond. I shall discover foreign shores, and name them all after me!' The General felt a warm glow as he imagined how famous he would become.

As the boat slowed, Nutmeg ran up on to the deck. She went to the railing, and stood by Tumtum's side, gazing out in dismay on the endless ocean of water. Looking back, they could still just see the children on the bank. But they were becoming smaller and smaller. The boat had already drifted well out of their reach. Nutmeg turned very pale.

'Turn us round, General,' Tumtum pleaded.

'We can't turn round now,' the General retorted. 'If we go back to the bank the children will catch us. And you don't want that, do you, Nutmouse?' He tightened his grip on the steering wheel, and stared straight ahead. He knew the Nutmouses were at his mercy, and he had an expression of intense mischief on his face.

Nutmeg looked back desperately at the bank. But it was far behind them now, and the children had become little dots in the distance. Gradually, the shore faded from sight too, and in every direction, as far as the eye could see, there was nothing but water.

'We are entering the unknown!' whooped the General, punching a fist in the air.

'This is madness. We've no compass, and no clean clothes, and virtually nothing left to eat,' Tumtum protested.

But the General had the scent of adventure in his nostrils; and nothing could stop him now. On and on he sailed, weaving *Bluebottle* through the dragonflies and the algae, towards where the sun glittered on a ceaseless horizon.

The Nutmouses begged him again and again to turn back. 'There's nothing out there, General. We could sail on forever, and never see dry land,' Tumtum said when they had been afloat nearly half an hour.

But the General did not hear him. He had picked up his field glasses, and was staring straight ahead, transfixed by something he had seen on the horizon. It was only a blur, and at first he fancied he might have been dreaming. But then, little by little, the object became sharper, until there could be no mistaking what it was.

For there, directly ahead of them, in those bleak, uncharted waters, lay an island. An unexplored island, upon which *he*, the great General Marchmouse, would be the first mouse ever to set foot.

I shall call it Marchmouse Island! he thought, feverishly. *My name will be on every map!*

He turned back to Tumtum and Nutmeg, cleared his lungs, and shouted:

'Land Ahoy!'

CHAPTER SIX

The children stood a long time on the bank, watching *Bluebottle* drift away. They had not seen the three mice on board, for they were hidden by the wooden railing encircling the deck.

Eventually, the boat reached the island, and bumped to a stop. 'You'll have to go in and get it,' Lucy said.

Arthur made a face. The water was full of weeds and you could not see the bottom. 'Why don't you go in?' he replied.

'Because it's not my boat. And I wouldn't even if it was. I remember Pa saying the water was very deep. You'd have to swim to reach the island. Just think—if you open your mouth, you might swallow a frog.'

Arthur shuddered. He wasn't going to risk that. 'So what shall we do? We can't just leave it here,' he said, for *Bluebottle* was one of his favourite toys.

'I wouldn't worry if I were you,' Lucy replied. 'It's bound to drift back to the bank eventually. We can come and check this afternoon. But now we'd better get a move on. We promised we'd be back for breakfast.'

Lucy suspected that their father would not notice if they broke this promise. But she wanted breakfast all the same.

'OK,' Arthur said reluctantly. 'But will you definitely come back with me this afternoon?'

'Of course,' Lucy said.

They walked together back to the campsite, and started packing everything away. They did not notice the Nutmouses' tent, nor their campfire, which was still burning away beneath the nettle clump, small as a penny.

*   *   *

Meanwhile, *Bluebottle*'s predicament was much worse than the children had feared. As she approached the island, the General had tried to steer her into a little pebbled cove he had spotted on the shore. But there was some litter drifting about, and when the boat was less than a ruler's length from the bank she had collided head on with a milk bottle, and gouged a hole in her hull.

The mice felt the deck heave as water started seeping into the hold. They had sprung a leak. It was a terrible disaster. But the General seemed remarkably unconcerned.

'Marchmouse Island!' he declared, blowing a kiss towards the shore. 'And all discovered by me!'

'General, our boat is going to sink,' Tumtum said pointedly.

'Oh, never mind that,' the General cried. 'We shall have plenty of time to build another one. Now, come on. Let's get out and explore!'

Tumtum looked exasperated. But when he and Nutmeg went below deck to inspect the damage, they found the Captain's cabin already flooding. There was nothing they could do. *Bluebottle* had been battered beyond repair.

They retrieved the hamper and hurried back upstairs. 'We're shipwrecked,' Nutmeg said miserably.

She turned a moment, and looked back across the vast pond. The mainland was far from sight, lost beyond the horizon.

And before them lay a wild, unknown shore. She shivered. Even the silence felt hostile to her now. She wondered if they would ever see Nutmouse Hall again.

'Cheer up, my dear lady, for we shall be shipwrecked in great style!' the General said cheerfully. 'We are the first settlers on this island, and we shall set the highest standards. We shall build a colossal villa—"Villa Colossus", we'll call it—and it shall have verandas and fountains, and fancy colonnades. And we shall dine every night on fresh tadpole fillets, roasted on an open fire!'

'Oh, poppycock,' Tumtum said crossly. 'The only thing we need to worry about is building a boat, so that we can all get home.'

'All in due course, Nutmouse. All in due course,' the General replied. 'Our first priority is to chart out the island, so that when we do return to our native land, we can tell everyone exactly what we've found. Imagine how astonished our friends will be to learn that there is a whole new country, right here, in The Pond!'

The General slung his rifle over his

arm, then he clambered over the side of the boat and slithered along the milk bottle to the shore. 'The first settlers have arrived!' he cried, marching on to dry land.

He could not see the rest of the island, for the cove was ringed with a tall forest of bracken. He picked his way over the pebbles, and dumped his rucksack on a patch of moss. 'We shall establish ourselves here. We can set up camp first, and explore later,' he declared.

'All right,' Tumtum said grudgingly, for if they were going to be stuck on the island overnight they would need somewhere to shelter. 'Nutmeg and I will gather some twigs, then we can make a lean-to,' he said.

'I want a villa, not a lean-to,' the General replied stubbornly. Tumtum sighed. The General was being very difficult. But then Nutmeg solved the problem.

'We shall make that your villa!' she declared, pointing to an ice cream tub washed up on the far side of the cove.

'It's pink!' the General protested.

But once they had dragged the tub

over to their campsite, and turned it upside down, even the General had to admit that it looked rather smart. It was tall and round, like a tower, and there would be ample room for three beds inside. Tumtum hacked out a door and two windows using the bread knife from the picnic hamper, then he carried three pebbles inside to use as chairs.

On the outside of the pot was the remains of a faded label that read 'Vanilla'. 'We shall call it "Villa Vanilla",' the General said. It wasn't big enough to be a Villa Colossus. They could make one of those later.

Presently, Tumtum lit a fire, and Nutmeg prepared a late lunch from the odds and ends left in the hamper. It was a meagre meal, for she rationed everything very strictly. They were each allowed one sausage roll, and half a centipede pasty, and a chocolate mint for pudding.

They were finished eating in no time.

'Well then, General,' Tumtum said. 'We had better start building a boat.'

'Not now, Nutmouse,' he replied. 'I'm going exploring first. We can begin our boring old boat-building tomorrow.'

'Well don't be long,' Tumtum said. 'And if you fall down a mole hole, don't expect us to come and rescue you.'

'Mole hole, pah! I tell you, we are the first rodents on this island. I can feel it in my bones,' General Marchmouse said confidently. Then he slung his rucksack over his shoulder and strode into the bracken.

*　　*　　*

The ferns were very thick, and it soon became so dark the General had to grope his way with his paws. But after a while the wood cleared, and he found himself at the foot of a steep bank, covered in cow parsley. He started climbing, hoisting himself up by the plant stems, until he came to a long flat ridge. He was right at the top, high above the level of the pond. He could see the whole island stretched before him.

And what a magnificent island it was! The coastline was wild and rugged, and full of pebbled cliffs, and there were jungles of thistles and bulrushes. In the middle of the island was a lake, more than half a metre long, surrounded by swathes of buttercups. The General peered through his field glasses, searching for any sign of habitation. But there was not a soul to be seen, not even a dragonfly. Everything was eerily still.

He took a swig of water from his hip flask, and prepared to press on towards the lake, hoping he might at least unearth an exotic beetle or two. But suddenly, in the corner of his eye, he saw something flickering—then all at once there was a brilliant flash of light on the far corner of the island.

He grabbed his field glasses and peered along the shore, trying to find where it had come from. But there was nothing there. He could just see the nettles rippling in the breeze.

He looked again, searching the rushes along the water's edge—and then suddenly a dark shape appeared through the lens. He steadied his paws, until he could see it clearly. It was a black ship, with grey sails, and the name *Lady Crossbones* painted in blood-red letters on its side.

The General reeled back in horror. He knew to whom that boat belonged. The Rats had arrived on Marchmouse Island.

CHAPTER SEVEN

The General ducked behind a buttercup, fearing he might be seen. Then he crouched there very still, staring at the ship through his field glasses.

It was the first time he had set eyes on *Lady Crossbones*. But like every mouse he knew her name, for she had inspired many a blood-curdling legend. She belonged to the Rats, who were the most feared rodents in the entire county. The Rats were not just any old rats. They were a small minority of rats, who gave themselves a capital 'R', and behaved especially badly.

They were pirates, which meant that all their nice things—their crystal glasses and their soup tureens and their silver candlesticks—had been robbed from other rodents' boats. As far as the Rats were concerned, robbing was a sport, and they prided themselves on being the very best at it.

Whenever they saw another boat coming, they would sail straight at it, then charge on board, howling and screeching, and firing their muskets in the air, and shouting, 'Your money or your life!' And if any hapless vole or field mouse refused to hand over his valuables, the Rats would throw him overboard and set alight to his boat. That's why everyone feared them.

There was a time when no mouse would dare go sailing on the stream, for fear of being attacked. But that was long ago. For the Rats had not been seen in these parts since the General had been a cadet. Everyone assumed they had moved on downstream, to terrorise another community.

But now they were back.

The General had seen many a chilling photograph of *Lady Crossbones*, but she looked much more sinister in real life. She was huge, three times the length of *Bluebottle*, and at her bow there was a figurehead of a snarling cat. She was anchored about a foot from the shore, beside a cove surrounded by thistles.

At first, the General could not see anyone on board. But then a trapdoor opened on the deck, and a big grey rat emerged. Almost at once, a black rat slithered out behind him. Then a brown rat appeared, then a white one; and then came a rat with only half a tail.

There were five Rats in all. The General swivelled the lens of his field glasses, until he could see them more clearly. They looked very menacing. Each was dressed in a black cape, with tall leather boots rising to his knees. Four of the Rats had red handkerchiefs tied round their heads. But the grey rat, who was clearly the captain, was a wearing a black felt hat, and he had a dragonfly perched on his shoulder.

All the rats were carrying swords. And when they spoke to each other, the General could see their fangs glinting in the sun.

When they were all gathered on the deck, two of the Rats lowered a thin raft down over the side of the ship. Then they all clambered overboard and squeezed into it, and began rowing in to the shore.

The General scrambled to his feet. He knew he must get back to camp at once, and warn the Nutmouses of what he had seen. As he tumbled back down the

70

bank, he could feel himself trembling. But now it was as much from anger as from fear.

'How *dare* those savages land on Marchmouse Island!' he raged. 'It is *my* island, and no ship may enter its shores without *my* permission! I wouldn't be surprised if they don't claim they got here first, and discovered the island before me. Well just let them try!'

He was so indignant he felt ready for anything. He would wage a war. He would shoot the Rats down from Villa Vanilla, and blow up their boat! It would be the greatest victory of his career.

But of course Tumtum might not play along with it. He was such a peace-loving mouse, he wouldn't like the idea one bit.

The General had been gone all afternoon, and the Nutmouses were very relieved to see him back. They fell on him with questions, wanting to know everything he had seen.

Little by little, the General told them about the wild shoreline, and the forest of thistles and the plains of buttercups and the glimmering lake—all theirs for the taking.

'It is a first-class island, a true jewel,' he concluded. 'If I were a businessmouse, I'd turn it into a holiday resort.'

'And you are quite sure there is no one else here?' Tumtum asked, for the General had seemed a little cagey on this matter.

'Well, no—er, that's to say, no one except—'

'Except who?' Tumtum interrupted.

'Oh, just a few other rodents,' the General said hastily. 'But, er, they don't live here, you see—no, no, they're just visiting. They've moored their ship in a cove on the opposite shore. I saw it when I climbed to the top of the hill.'

'But what good fortune!' Nutmeg cried, surprised the General had held back such vital information. 'We must go to them at once, and ask them for a lift back across The Pond.'

'Er, I'm not sure that's such a good idea . . .' the General stammered. 'You see, they are . . . well, they're—'

'Who are they?' Tumtum asked sharply, wondering what the General was trying to hide.

The General looked at the ground, and scuffled the earth with his shoe. He suddenly felt a prickle of shame for having landed his friends in such danger. There was a long silence. Then he said sheepishly, 'They are the Rats.'

'*The Rats?* Are you sure?' Tumtum asked. 'I thought they'd moved downstream.'

'Yes, I'm sure,' the General said reluctantly expecting Tumtum to be very cross. 'They arrived on that infamous old ship of theirs, *Lady Crossbones*. There are five of them, so far as I could see.'

The Nutmouses looked stunned. It was such dreadful news, it took a while to sink in.

'Now look here, my friends,' the General began, trying to jolly them up a bit. 'This is *our* island, and we can't let those vagabonds frighten us. We shall make Villa Vanilla our fortress, and fight to the last!'

'*Us?* Fight the Rats? Don't be a fool, General, we'd be eaten alive,' Tumtum snapped. He could have boxed the General's ears for landing them in such trouble—but luckily for the General he had more important things to do.

He looked around him, quickly taking stock of their situation. They had no boat to escape in, and no time to build one, for the Rats were sure to explore the island soon.

'We must hide,' Nutmeg said anxiously. And Tumtum agreed.

'Yes. We'll have to bury all traces of this camp, then take cover in the bracken,' he said. 'With any luck they'll sail away in a day or two.'

Tumtum started throwing earth on the fire, while Nutmeg hurriedly replaced their picnic things in the hamper.

The General stood and watched. 'I am going to stay here and defend my villa,' he announced stubbornly.

'But you haven't a chance, General,' Tumtum said. 'They'll pelt it with pebbles, and knock it down flat, and when you come running out squealing they'll pounce on you, and tear you to shreds. Now come on. Let's make ourselves scarce.'

'I shall *not* hide! You can run away if you like, but I'm staying here. I am an officer in the Royal Mouse Army, and I shall face them like a mouse!'

To prove his intent, the General picked up his rifle, and slung it over his shoulder. He had no bullets left, for he had used the last round on the macaroni cheese. But the gun felt reassuring all the same.

'You do know that the Rats make their prisoners walk the gangplank?' Tumtum said, remembering the stories his father had told him when he was little.

But not even a threat as terrible as this would change the General's mind. And in the end, after a good deal more threatening and pleading, Tumtum and Nutmeg were forced to go and hide on their own.

They took the hamper with them, but they gave the General more than half the rations, including the last sausage roll. All the same, they felt wretched leaving him. When they reached the edge of the cove they turned to wave him goodbye, but he was busy barricading Villa Vanilla with pebbles.

'The Rats are sure to capture him,' Nutmeg said forlornly.

'Well it's no good us being captured

too,' Tumtum replied. 'Anyway, I reckon he'll feel less brave when it gets dark, and come running after us.'

'Hmmm. I hope you're right,' Nutmeg said. But she was not so sure. 'Oh, if only we had a boat, then we could sail away from this beastly island.'

'I told you, dear, we'll make one,' Tumtum said.

'But how? We don't know anything about boat-building. And we haven't even got a saw.'

Tumtum wished he could think of something reassuring to say. But they both knew that the situation was very bleak. They walked on silently, deep in thought. As they were about to enter the bracken Nutmeg turned and looked back at The Pond, searching the water as if by some miracle a friendly boat might suddenly have appeared. But all she could see was some rubbish washed up on the bank—an old wine bottle, and some ancient bailer twine which had drifted from the farm buildings further down the stream. Beyond it the water was empty. There was nothing moving save for the tiny ripples buffeting The Pond's surface.

Then she noticed that since they had arrived on the island the breeze had changed direction. It was blowing away from them now, back towards the far-off bank from which they had come. She stood very still, watching the water. Then she looked back at the wine bottle, studying it more closely. It was empty, and its label had been washed off. But it still had its cork.

She bit her lip. She had thought of a plan.

'Tumtum,' she said suddenly. 'I've had an idea.'

'What is it, dear?' Tumtum asked hopefully. He knew that Nutmeg's ideas weren't always sensible. But given the crisis they were in, he felt that any idea was better than none.

'We can write Arthur and Lucy a letter, telling them that we're in trouble, and asking them to send out another toy boat to rescue us,' Nutmeg explained, clapping her hands with glee.

'*Write to them?*' Tumtum replied. 'But my dear wife, you seem to forget that we are shipwrecked on an island. There is no postal service here.' He looked at

Nutmeg tenderly. He supposed that all the heat and excitement must be making her muddled.

But Nutmeg wasn't muddled a bit.

'That will be our postal service,' she said, pointing to the rubbish on the bank. 'We can put a letter in that wine bottle, then push it out on to The Pond and let it drift back to the shore. Look, you see the way the tide's moving; it's sure to get there. And then when the children come back looking for *Bluebottle*, which they're certain to do, they might just notice it.'

'Goodness,' Tumtum said, trying to take it all in. 'But how will we seal it?'

'Look,' Nutmeg replied triumphantly. 'It's still got its cork.'

'Well, I suppose it's worth a try,' Tumtum said. 'But what shall we write on? We'll need a very big piece of paper, if there's to be any chance of the children seeing it.'

'There,' she said, pointing towards an old paper bag caught in the grass on the bank. 'We can write on that.'

'Well, I suppose it will do,' he said. 'And have we anything to write with?'

'Look in your pockets, dear,' Nutmeg replied. 'You've usually a pen buried somewhere.'

There followed an anxious moment as Tumtum emptied out his jacket pockets, where an assortment of boiled sweets and paper clips had gathered.

'Here!' he said finally, pulling out a nibbled black biro.

They flattened the bag on the ground, then Nutmeg took the pen and knelt down to compose an SOS.

Tumtum stood over her, reading out loud as she wrote:

The Island, The Pond

Dear Arthur and Lucy,
I accidentally got swept away this morning in your boat—but alas she collided with a milk bottle, and is now damaged beyond repair, leaving me shipwrecked on the island. I am so terribly sorry, my dears, but I do not think your beloved Bluebottle *will ever sail again. I will try to replace her in time. But for the moment I must ask your help. You see, I am in some*

danger, because a band of pirates has arrived here too. They are savage creatures, who steal and bite and carry swords, so perhaps you would be kind enough to help me escape before they find me. I need you to find another toy boat, and float it out to the island as soon as you can, so that I can sail home in it, and come and visit you again in the attic.
Love,
Nutmeg.

She did not mention Tumtum, as in her previous letters to the children she had only ever referred to herself. As far as Arthur and Lucy were concerned, they had one fairy in their attic, not two.

'Good. Now let's get it in the bottle,' Tumtum said impatiently. They had been dallying in the open for a long time, and he was anxious to get under cover.

They rolled the letter into a cylinder, and carried it to the water's edge. Then they wrenched the cork from the neck of the bottle, and eased the letter inside. When they had finished, they pressed the cork back in as tightly as they could.

They pushed as though their lives depended on it, sweat pouring down their coats.

'There, that must be watertight now,' Tumtum said finally.

When everything was in place, the Nutmouses both braced themselves against the side of the bottle, and pushed on it with all their might, until finally it rolled down the bank, and plopped into the water.

They waited a moment to see if it would drift out from the shore. But then suddenly they heard a terrible noise coming from the other side of the island. It was the sound of braying and shrieking —then a piercing squeal, like a creature being pounced on.

'Come on!' Tumtum said, tugging Nutmeg by the arm. 'The Rats are on the move.'

CHAPTER EIGHT

Towards the end of the afternoon, Arthur and Lucy set out for The Pond, hoping to get their boat back. But in the last few hours water had been steadily seeping into *Bluebottle*'s hold, and by the time the children arrived she had sunk without trace.

'She's gone,' Arthur said miserably.

'She can't have gone,' Lucy said. 'She's probably just drifted round the island. Come on. Let's go and look.'

But when they reached the other side of The Pond it was not *Bluebottle* they saw, but *Lady Crossbones*, lying black and motionless by the island shore.

She was nestled in among the rushes, but they could see her quite clearly. They stood in silence a moment, dazzled by her grey sails and her cold beauty.

'Who do you think it belongs to?' Lucy asked eventually.

'I don't know. But with a name like *Lady Crossbones* it must be a pirate ship,' Arthur said. 'And look!' he gasped. 'It's even got a gangplank!' He felt his heart quicken. It looked much more real than any of the toy pirate ships he had seen.

There was nothing stirring on the deck. But they could see the Rats' lantern hanging from the mast. And there was light coming from one of the portholes.

'Maybe it sunk *Bluebottle*,' Arthur said.

'Don't be stupid,' Lucy replied. 'Toy boats don't sink each other.'

'But this boat doesn't look like a toy,' Arthur said. 'It looks real.'

Lucy shivered. It did look real—and it had a sinister air. Its owner must be here somewhere. She looked round The Pond fearfully, as if expecting some vile creature suddenly to burst out from the water. But everything was very still.

Then she noticed a small gleam of light, as the sun caught on something tucked into the rushes just below where she was standing.

Lucy knelt down on the bank, and hurriedly brushed aside the plants, wondering what it could be. But then she saw that it was just an old bottle. *It must have been washed up the stream*, she thought, and yet something about it caught her eye.

She leaned down and picked it out of the water. 'Look at this,' she said, showing the bottle to Arthur.

He shrugged. It didn't look very interesting.

Lucy brushed the glass with her sleeve. 'There's a piece of paper inside it,' she said.

'*A piece of paper?*' Arthur said, suddenly intrigued. 'Here, let's have a look.'

Lucy passed it to him, and he held the bottle close up to his face, and peered inside.

He pulled out the cork, and shook out the piece of brown paper. Then he unrolled it, and held it flat.

The writing was too small for the children to read, and the ink had become smudged. But they recognised the strange, loopy pattern of the letters, and knew at once that it was in Nutmeg's hand.

They both gasped. Whatever was Nutmeg doing sending them a letter in a bottle? That meant she must be on the

island. But why? Could it be that *she* had something to do with the sinister pirate ship?

'We must work out what it says—she probably knows what's happened to *Bluebottle*,' Lucy said urgently.

'Try this,' Arthur said, pulling a small magnifying glass from his penknife. It was not very strong, but when Lucy held it over the paper she could make out most of what was written. She read the letter out loud to Arthur, guessing the words which were too faint to see.

Arthur listened in astonishment. When he heard his boat had sunk he looked close to tears. 'So it was Nutmeg who took *Bluebottle*!' he said in dismay. 'Well she can't be much good at sailing if she let it sink. Now we'll never get it back.'

'Why are you still worrying about *Bluebottle*?' Lucy asked scathingly. 'It's Nutmeg that matters now. Have you got another boat we can use to rescue her?'

'Not really,' he said, suddenly regretting his reaction. 'There's only the plastic one in the bathroom, and that leaks.'

'Then we'll have to make one,' Lucy

said. 'There must be something at home we can use. Come on. If we hurry we can get back here before supper.'

The children ran back to Rose Cottage, and started turning out the kitchen cupboards, looking for something boat-like. There was a bread tin, but it was too rusty; and there was a yogurt pot, but that was too deep. There was a wooden salad bowl which might have worked, but a woodworm had eaten through it.

Then Lucy found an old margarine tub, which was being used to keep elastic bands in. 'That'll do fine,' Arthur said. 'It will be just Nutmeg's size.'

What they did next was very clever. They attached two twigs in a cross to make a mast, then tied on one of Mr Mildew's handkerchiefs for a sail, and stuck it in the tub with Blu-Tack. Then they put in two teaspoons for Nutmeg to use as oars, in case there was no breeze.

When they had finished, they ran straight back to The Pond. They had been gone nearly two hours, and the dusk was gathering. But the pirate ship had not moved.

'I hope we're not too late,' Lucy said,

looking at it with apprehension.

'I wouldn't have thought so,' Arthur replied confidently. 'It's getting dark, so you'd have thought the pirates would have stopped pirating for today. And by the time they start up again tomorrow, Nutmeg will have escaped in our boat.'

They walked to the water's edge and launched the margarine tub from the bank opposite the ship. Arthur poked it as far as it would go with a stick. Then they stood and watched as the breeze played in its sail, nudging it towards the cove where *Bluebottle* had sunk.

CHAPTER NINE

Back on Marchmouse Island, events were developing at quite a pace.

The Rats had roasted a frog for their dinner, and they were full of rich food and high spirits. As the night drew in, they began rampaging across the island, slashing the heads off dandelions.

Tumtum and Nutmeg lay trembling in the bracken, buried deep under a pile of ferns. They were well hidden, but they were frightened the Rats would sniff them out. Nutmeg wished she had applied less perfume that morning.

The Rats came closer and closer, until they were so near the Nutmouses could hear the leaves rustling under their feet. When they were but a few centimetres from where the mice were hiding, they stopped a moment, wondering which way to go—then they gave another cheer and rampaged on.

The Nutmouses waited until the wood had gone quiet again. Then they poked their noses out of the ferns, and took a deep breath.

'That was close,' Tumtum commented.

'They sounded the most awful savages,' Nutmeg said. 'I do hope the General doesn't do anything too silly. If he goes taking potshots at them from his villa they'll tear him to shreds.'

'He wouldn't dare,' Tumtum said confidently. 'He'll be feeling much less brave now that we've left him on his own. I'll bet the last hair on my tail that he's gone into hiding too.'

If only he had. For then the Nutmouses' ordeal might have ended rather sooner. But the General was not hiding. Far from it. At that particular moment, he was standing outside Villa Vanilla, stoking his campfire, and roasting a snail for his supper.

And he was thinking the same defiant old thoughts—such as, *I'll show the Rats who owns this island!* and, *Hah! They won't get rid of me!*

But trouble arrived sooner than he might have expected. For by now the Rats had emerged from the bracken, and were clambering up the bank behind the starlit cove. When they reached the top, they sat down a moment to admire the view. They were very still, with the dragonfly perched motionless on the Captain's shoulder.

Then they saw the General's campfire flickering on the beach.

They suddenly jumped to their feet, enraged and astonished. Until then, they had believed they had the whole island to themselves.

'Who the devil's down there?' snarled the Captain, whose name was Captain Pong. He grabbed his telescope, and glared down the bank. His dragonfly clung to his shoulder, giving an angry flap of its wings. It was a brilliant night, and the Captain could see Villa Vanilla gleaming a soft pink in the moonlight. Then he saw the General, illuminated by the campfire.

'Well I'm damned. It's a mouse!' he said.

'*A mouse?*' the others cried. 'How dare there be a mouse! This is our island. It's *Rat* Island. Let's see him off!'

'Hang on a minute,' Captain Pong snapped, twizzling his lens to get a better look. 'I know that mouse. It's General Marchmouse!'

93

'General Marchmouse? It can't be!' the others said. The Captain gave them each a turn with the telescope, so they could see for themselves. And then there could be no doubting it.

None of the Rats had met General Marchmouse before. But they recognised him at once, for he was very famous. They had seen his picture time and again in *The Mouse Times*, and there had been posters of him on some of the boats they had robbed. Not so long ago, he had even had his face on a stamp.

The General was a legend of his time. And now here he was, cooking his supper on their beach!

They all sucked in their breath. The Rats were very jealous of the General, because he was the only rodent with a reputation as big as theirs.

'Ha! Who does he think he is?' the black rat snarled.

'Stupid little squirt,' snorted the rat with half a tail.

And going through all their minds was the same nasty thought: *here was a chance to bring the General down a peg or two*.

'Let's tie him up and paint him purple!' said one.

'Let's make him walk the plank!' said another.

'Let's make him ride a frog!' said a third—and so they went on, suggesting more and more horrible things they might do.

'Quiet!' the Captain hissed, fearing the General might hear them. 'Come on, we'll take him unawares.'

The crew stopped squeaking, and slithered silently down the bank. When they reached the cove, they hid behind a clump of nettles, watching as the General turned his supper on the spit. Then they crept up to Villa Vanilla and crouched in the shadows, waiting to pounce.

* * *

The General was taking his time, for he liked his meat well cooked. Eventually, when the snail was brown all over, he took it from the fire and made back towards the villa. His mind was wandering, recalling all the battles he had won, and he did not hear the Rats sniggering. But as he put out his hand to open the door he felt a cold paw on his neck.

'Gotcha!' the Captain said.

The General kicked and nipped and squealed, but he was no match for five rats. After only the briefest of struggles, he was knocked out cold. Then he was slung over the brown rat's shoulder and carried back across the island to the ship.

It was perhaps just as well the General was unconscious, for it was a long hike, up hill and down dale, and through a swamp and a thistle forest.

Had the General been awake, the Rats would have made him walk. And he would have hated every step. But as it was he was carried along like a sack of Smarties. He was still unconscious when the Rats heaved him on to the ship, and locked him in a cabin below deck.

When the General finally came round he felt very stiff. He sat up painfully, trying to work out what had happened to him. He was on a bare wooden floor, in a small room, furnished with a stool and a bookcase full of silver plates and candlesticks. On the wall above him was a porthole, letting in a pale dawn light.

In a rush of shame, he remembered being ambushed outside Villa Vanilla, and realised the Rats must have imprisoned him on their ship. It was a glum awakening.

He stood up and rattled the door shouting, 'Let me out!'—but no one came. He shouted until he was worn out, then he collapsed on the floor and sat with his head in his paws, brooding miserably.

Finally, he heard a key in the lock. As he jumped to his feet, the door was flung open and the black rat and the brown rat walked in.

The black rat had a ring through his nose, and the brown rat had only one fang. They both had scars on their faces which made them look even more ferocious.

'Sit on the stool,' the black rat said. And the General did, because the rat was much bigger than him. Then both rats stood in front of him, looking at him very hard, and asking lots of questions. This was called an interrogation, and it was not at all pleasant.

'How did you get here?' the black rat snarled, leaning over the General so close their noses were almost touching.

'I arrived on *Bluebottle*,' the General trembled.

'Where is she now?'

'She has sunk. She collided with a milk bottle, and sprang a leak.'

'Who else was with you?'

'No one,' the General lied.

'Were there any valuables on board?' the brown rat drooled.

The General was so nervous he started to babble. 'Valuables? Gracious, no. *Bluebottle* was rather basic, you know. The only thing of any possible value was Mr Nutmouse's silver picnicking crockery—it was rather fancy, you know, blue and white, with impressions of bumble bees . . . Anyway, he and Mrs Nutmouse took that with them when they went off to hide in the—'

The General suddenly realised what he had done, and clapped a paw to his mouth. 'Oops,' he said.

But it was too late. At the mention of Tumtum's name the Rats' ears had gone as stiff as cardboard. For the Nutmouses

99

were rumoured to be fabulously rich, with a huge mansion full of expensive furniture. They should surely demand a king's ransom if they kidnapped Mr and Mrs Nutmouse, of Nutmouse Hall!

'Where are they?' the Rats growled.

'I don't know,' the General gulped.

'Yes you do! Now tell us where they went to hide!'

'I tell you, I don't know!'

'Yes you do!'

'No I don't!'

'Yes you do!'

'No I don't!'

There was no danger of the General giving in, of course, because a General would never betray a friend. But nonetheless, his voice had started to waver.

Then the door opened again, and the other Rats appeared.

'What's going on?' Captain Pong asked, giving the General a menacing glare.

'He sailed here with Mr Nutmouse— you know, that stinking rich fellow, who inherited Nutmouse Hall,' the brown rat explained. 'Their ship was sunk, and now

Nutmouse and his wife are hiding somewhere on the island.' The rat paused, and pointed at the General accusingly. 'He knows where they are. *But he won't tell us!*'

'Then throw him overboard,' Captain Pong said.

'Throw him overboard!' the others cried, delighted with this plan.

The General leapt from his seat, punching and squealing, but he was overpowered in no time. They tied his paws behind his back and marched him up to the deck, then hoisted him on to the gangplank.

It was a thin, springy gangplank, and it struck the General that it went on a very long way. He could see the tip flapping.

'Go on!' the Rats sneered, prodding him in the back with a candlestick. 'Walk!'

The General looked down at the dark water, and fancied he could see the shadow of an enormous fish. He felt his legs wobble. He could hear the Rats chanting—'Walk! Walk! Walk!'— but their voices had become faint and echoey, as if coming from a cavern far

102

away. The General had never known fear like this.

He could not go on.

'Oh, please, Sirs!' he quaked, his face reddening with shame. 'The Nutmouses are in the bracken wood!'

CHAPTER TEN

Had the Rats been truly horrible, they might have made General Marchmouse walk the gangplank all the same. But in most creatures there is a shred of mercy. So once the General had given them the information they required, they pulled him down, cuffed his ears, and locked him back in his cabin.

The General watched from his porthole as the Rats clambered back into their raft, and rowed to the shore. He could hear them as they made their way across the island, screeching blood-thirstily as they went to track Tumtum and Nutmeg down.

He knew there was no hope for the Nutmouses now. Soon they would be prisoners too, and it was all *his* fault for betraying them. He sat on his stool, seized with remorse. It gave him a hot, tickly feeling to think how cross Tumtum would be.

Before long, two dreadful squeals rose from the depths of the island, and he knew his friends had been captured.

Presently, he heard the Rats clattering back on to the deck.

'Lock them up below!' one of them shouted. And next thing the door to the General's cabin was opened, and Tumtum and Nutmeg were flung inside.

They were a sorry spectacle. Their clothes were torn and scuffed, and they had burrs in their hair. And Tumtum's watch was broken. But their spirits were still intact.

'These Rats are savages!' Nutmeg cried. 'You should have seen what they've done to Villa Vanilla, General. They've battered down the walls, and gnawed a big hole in the roof. Oh, it's a pitiful mess. And they stole our last slice of ginger cake—and smashed the picnic glasses!'

'Did they ambush you in the bracken?' the General asked sheepishly. But to his relief Tumtum did not suspect him of betrayal.

'They caught us in the cove, just as we were trying to sail away in the margarine tub,' he replied. 'If they had only arrived a minute later, we'd have been able to escape.'

'*The Margarine Tub*? Who's she?' the General asked, thinking this a curious name for a boat.

'She is a margarine tub, as her name suggests,' Nutmeg said.

'But a cut above most margarine tubs,' Tumtum added proudly. 'She has a fine cotton sail, and oars made of solid steel.'

The General looked even more bewildered. But then the Nutmouses started at the beginning, and told him all about the SOS they had sent to the children; and how they had crept down to the cove that morning, as soon as it was light, and found the margarine tub washed up on the pebbles, like an answer to a prayer.

'And we were just pushing it out to water, about to set sail, when the Rats sprang out of the bushes, shouting, "Who goes there?" ' Nutmeg went on. 'And then they searched the boat, and found a letter in it from Arthur and Lucy. It was clearly addressed to me, but the Rats read it all the same. And it was just an innocent letter, explaining that I should be careful with the sail, as it was attached with Blu-Tack, and might wobble a bit.

'But of course the Rats made a terrible fuss about it, and wanted to know who Arthur and Lucy were. So we told them they were only human children, who meant no harm. And then the Rats' eyes went all narrow and greedy, and they asked us if the children were rich. And Tumtum laughed, and said, "Oh, dear me, no. They're not rich at all. Quite the contrary: they're so poor, they can't afford jam for their bread." But the Rats wouldn't believe it. And they sent the boat back to the shore, with another letter in it—a letter from them to Arthur and Lucy. And . . . and—'

'And what did the Rats' letter say?' the General asked impatiently. But Nutmeg had started sobbing, and couldn't go on.

'They informed Arthur and Lucy that they had taken Nutmeg hostage,' Tumtum said. 'And they said that if the children send the boat back to the island by tonight, filled to the brim with gold, then they will let her go. But if the Rats do not receive the gold before darkness falls, they will make her walk the gangplank.'

'And what about you and me?' the General asked self-centredly.

'We don't feature in the letters, because the children don't know we're here,' Tumtum replied. 'But the Rats advised me that if they make Nutmeg walk the gangplank, they'll make us walk it too.'

The General grimaced. 'Do you think the children will meet their demands?' he asked.

'How can they?' Nutmeg cried. 'They haven't got any gold. Not a pound coin between them.'

'In that case we're in a spot of bother,' the General said.

* * *

Lucy woke early that morning, expecting to find that Nutmeg had visited the attic in the night. But the midnight feast of milk and biscuit crumbs that the children had left out in the doll's house was untouched. And there was no note from her on the chest of drawers.

'Arthur, wake up,' she cried. 'She hasn't been here.'

'She's probably still making her way back from The Pond,' Arthur grunted, pulling the covers over his head. 'Now, go away and let me sleep. It's not fair being woken up this early when it's half-term.'

'Oh, *please*,' Lucy said. 'I want to go down to The Pond now. If we can find the margarine tub then at least we'll know if Nutmeg got away from the island.' She got up and opened the curtains. It was already light. 'Come on. If we go now we can be back for breakfast.'

'Oh, all right,' Arthur said, for he was curious too. The children got dressed and tiptoed downstairs so as not to wake their father. Then they let themselves out of the garden door and ran across the meadow.

It felt cooler today, and The Pond was scattered with a thin, feathery mist. The pirate ship had not moved. It was still lying motionless beside the island, its deck deserted and its portholes unlit. But the margarine tub was nowhere to be seen.

'It can't have just disappeared,' Lucy said.

'Maybe it's sunk,' Arthur suggested glumly.

'Of course it hasn't sunk,' Lucy said. *Bluebottle* sinking was bad enough. The margarine tub couldn't sink too. It would be too much bad luck.

She started round the bank to look again, brushing aside the rushes with her hands. And then suddenly she saw the little boat floating on the water, just a few yards from where she was standing. It had appeared as if by magic. It had mist in its sails, and it looked grey and ghostly.

There was no one on board.

'Arthur, look. It's here,' she called. 'Can you get it?'

'Hang on,' he replied. He found a long stick, then he lay on the grass, and gently pulled the margarine tub into the bank.

Lucy lay down beside him and reached it out of the water.

'There's something in it,' she said, taking out a tiny tin, as small as a thimble. (It belonged to the Captain. He always carried a tin in his knapsack, in case he found a delicious bug he wanted to take back to the ship to fry for his supper.) Lucy prised off the lid with her thumbnail. And inside the tin she found

a piece of paper, folded several times.

'It must be another letter from Nutmeg,' Arthur said. But the children got a fright when they unravelled it, for the writing looked very sinister. The page was smudged with black ink, and the letters were all botched and coarse. It was quite different to Nutmeg's hand.

'What does it say?' Arthur asked.

Lucy read it out to him. The Rats' handwriting was much bigger than Nutmeg's, so she did not need a magnifying glass to decipher it.

Rats Island
The Pond

To Arthur and Lucy,

Ur boat arived to late to save yor belovid Nutmeg. Weve taken her prisona, and were goin to show her wot hapins to any1 who tresparsis on R island. We wil sale out to were The Pond is deepist, and were there R giant fish in the waters. Then we will make her walk the gangplank, wiv her paws tide behind her back.

But if U are good children, and return The Margarine Tub to the island bye nightfal, filed to its brim wiv gold, then we wil set Nutmeg free, and let her sale back to the shoor. But rememba, we must get the gold by nightfal. Or U wil neva sea Nutmeg again.
From,
The Rats.

Arthur and Lucy were stunned. It was a very frightening letter to receive.

'They can't really be rats,' Arthur said. 'Rats can't write.'

'Well these rats can hardly write—look at their spelling,' Lucy said. 'But whoever they are we've got to get Nutmeg back before they do something awful to her.'

'But what can we do? We haven't got any gold to send them.'

'Then we'll have to tell Pa. Maybe he can swim out to the island and rescue her.'

'Don't be silly. Can you imagine Pa swimming? I shouldn't think he's ever been swimming in his life. And I hardly think he's going to throw himself into

114

The Pond in order to rescue a fairy who's been captured by rats. If we tell him that, he'll think we're just being silly.'

Lucy looked thoughtful. Arthur was right, their father would never believe their story. No one would believe it. It was much too strange. They were going to have to rescue Nutmeg themselves. One way or another, they needed to find some gold.

Then Arthur had an idea. 'Listen, you remember those chocolates that Aunt Ivy gave us at Christmas—the dark ones with goo in the middle?' he said excitedly.

Lucy nodded. She had tasted them and they had made her feel quite sick. They contained a disgusting syrupy substance called liqueur, which made her eyes water, and her throat sting. Chocolate liqueurs are very potent. If you eat too many, you start to feel drunk. But they are so revolting, not even the greediest person would want more than one.

No one had liked Aunt Ivy's chocolate liqueurs. So they had been sitting in the larder since Boxing Day, gathering dust.

'What about them?' Lucy said.

'Well, you remember what they looked like? Each one was wrapped in gold paper, and shaped like a brick. If we pack them all into the margarine tub, the pirates will think we've sent them a cargo of gold bullion!'

Lucy thought this was a wonderful plan. 'And we can write them a letter, saying we'll send over a second load as soon as we've got Nutmeg back,' she said cleverly. 'That way they'll be sure to keep to their side of the bargain. Come on, quick! Let's go and find them.'

Lucy picked up the margarine tub and they ran back to Rose Cottage. Then they took the chocolates from the larder and polished each one with a tea towel until it shone. They packed them into the boat two layers deep. And then Lucy found a piece of paper, and sat down at the kitchen to write the pirates a letter.

Dear Rats,

We are sending you these bricks of gold as a ransom. In return you must release Nutmeg AT ONCE, and let her use the boat to return to the shore. If you let her go tonight, we will send you a second cargo of gold in the morning. But if you keep her prisoner, we won't send you anything else, ever.

From,
Arthur and Lucy Mildew,
Rose Cottage.

Lucy folded the letter tightly, and wedged it beside the mast. Then they went straight back to The Pond. Lucy carried the margarine tub, covering it with both hands to make sure the chocolates didn't fall out.

They could see signs of life on *Lady Crossbones*. There was a wisp of smoke coming from a little stove on the deck, and a black flag had been raised on the mast. The children stood on the opposite bank, and pushed the margarine tub out on to the water.

'Now all we can do is wait,' Lucy said.

CHAPTER ELEVEN

The mice spent a horrible day locked up in their cabin. They were given nothing for lunch, and tea was just a piece of cheese—the sort of stale, rubbery cheese used in mousetraps. It was supper time now, but no supper had been served.

'If we don't escape soon we'll starve,' Tumtum said gloomily.

'I told you, escape is out of the question,' the General replied sharply. 'Even if we managed to break out of this cabin, our only hope of getting away would be to jump overboard. And then we might be eaten by fish.'

'Well I'd take a chance on it,' Nutmeg said. She had been away from Nutmouse Hall for two whole nights, and she was so homesick she felt she would risk anything to get back—even an encounter with a carp.

But the General had been badly shaken by his experience on the gangplank that morning, and was feeling less brave than usual. 'We must wait and see if the children come up with the ransom money,' he said. 'This is no time for foolish heroics.'

Tumtum was tempted to point out that if it hadn't been for the General's foolish heroics last night, when he had been so determined to defend Villa Vanilla, they might not have been captured at all. But he didn't.

'There is no way the children will raise the ransom,' he said instead. 'Last time I crawled into their piggy bank, it only had five pence in it. And five pence pieces are made of silver, not gold. Anyway, it will be dark soon. Our time's running out.'

The General shrugged. 'If no ransom arrives, we shall just have to negotiate with the Rats as best we can. Perhaps you can offer them Nutmouse Hall in exchange for our release,' he suggested.

Tumtum looked at him scornfully. *Give the Rats Nutmouse Hall?* he thought. *The house his great-great-great grandfather had built!* He would never do that.

And Tumtum was about to say as much. But then Nutmeg looked out of the porthole and let out a cry:

120

'The children have sent the boat back! And it *is* full of gold! Oh, Tumtum, look! It really is!'

Tumtum and the General rushed to the window and saw the margarine tub floating towards them with its cotton sail billowing in the wind. There was no one on board, just a great heap of gold bullion, glinting in the twilight. It was a strange and wonderful sight. The tub was heavily laden, and it had taken it the best part of the day to drift this far.

It did not take long for the Rats, who were eating supper on the deck, to notice it too. Their jaws dropped. At best, they had expected that the children might send them a few gold coins. But there was enough treasure here for them all to retire on.

'We'll never have to rob another boat again,' the brown rat dribbled.

In his mind's eye, each rat pictured the new life he would lead. A life of palaces, and hot baths, and soft beds, and long lie-ins, and banquets that went on and on. Oh, it would be a fine thing to be rich!

'Come on. Let's pull her in,' Captain

Pong said. The mice watched from the porthole as the Rats rowed out to the tub in a raft, then carefully looped a rope around the mast, and started towing it back to the shore.

They went very slowly, fearful one of the gold bricks might topple from the pile. When they reached the bank they dragged the margarine tub out of the water and rested it in the mud. Then they all gathered round it, looking rather tense. The gold was the most beautiful sight they had ever seen. But a sense of rivalry had developed between them, with each rat already fussing about whether he'd get his fair share.

'Don't touch it!' Captain Pong rasped, sensing a fight might break out. 'I'll count the bricks. And *I'll* decide who gets what.'

This caused alarm, for Captain Pong was not best known for his sense of fair play. But he had a paw placed meaningfully on his sword. So the other Rats hesitated to challenge him.

The Captain leaned over the tub, and tried to lift one of the bricks to see how heavy it was. It felt like concrete, for the chocolates were very stale. The others watched avidly as he raised it with both arms—then they gave a greedy cheer when they saw the second layer of bullion underneath.

'Hang on, what's this?' the Captain said, seeing the children's letter peeking out from the wrappers. He dumped his chocolate back on the pile and yanked the letter free. Then he laid it flat on the ground and stood at the bottom of the page, reading it out loud.

The Rats sucked in their breath as they heard the children's offer:

. . . If you let her go tonight, we will send you a second cargo of gold in the morning. But if you keep her prisoner, we won't send you anything else, ever . . .

'More gold!' they said dreamily. They were beginning to feel dizzy. At this rate, they would be the richest rats in the whole world.

'Well then. We'd better hurry up and unload this stuff, then let Mrs Nutmouse go,' the Captain said. And everyone

124

agreed, for they didn't want to miss out on a chance like this.

'What about Mr Nutmouse and the General?' asked the white rat, who spoke in a much squeakier voice than the others. 'The children make no mention of them. If we keep them hostage we might be able to demand a third load of gold later on.'

Captain Pong considered this for a moment. The prospect of a third load was certainly tempting. But he was worried Nutmeg might not be able to manage the margarine tub on her own. And if she capsized and drowned while crossing The Pond, there would be no more gold at all.

'Nah,' he said eventually. 'Let 'em all go. The wind will be against them. She'll need the gents to help her row.'

'Good riddance to them,' the other Rats said, for they were sick and tired of taking the prisoners lumps of cheese.

'So where shall we hide all this gold?' the black rat asked. 'It weighs a ton. It's going to be an awful sweat hauling it all up on to the ship.'

'We'll need a pulley. It will be hard

work, that's for sure,' the brown rat said.

'All right, all right. Let's not worry about that now,' said the Captain, who hated work of any kind. 'We can take it on to the ship tomorrow, once the second load's arrived. We can leave it here for now. It's not as though there's anyone to steal it.'

'But we can't just leave it out in the open. The birds might take it,' the black rat said.

Captain Pong muttered crossly. But the black rat was right, the treasure had to be moved. They all looked round for somewhere sheltered. Then the Captain pointed to a small cave at the rear of the cove, formed where two stones had toppled against each other.

'We can move it in there,' he said. 'It will be perfectly safe for a day or two.' He turned to the white rat. 'You. Go back to the ship and fetch the prisoners. The rest of us will stay here and unload.'

So the white rat rowed back to the ship in the raft, while the other rats started hauling the gold out of the margarine tub and lugging it across to the cave. When they had moved about half of the treasure, the white rat returned to the beach with the Nutmouses and the General.

'Get out,' he squeaked, bumping the raft to a stop against a pebble. The mice clambered nervously on to the beach, where they were addressed by Captain Pong.

'Those children of yours have met our demands, so when we've finished unloading our gold you can sail this margarine tub home,' he said mercifully. 'I only needed to release Mrs Nutmouse—but I have decided to let you all go.' It made him feel very powerful setting them free.

'Oh, how generous you are, Captain!' Nutmeg cried. She was so happy she could have kissed him.

But then there was a sudden shriek—and looking round they saw the brown rat trip head over tail on a twig. The gold brick that he had been carrying fell from his paws and crashed against a pebble.

'Careful! You'll dent it,' the Captain snarled. But something much worse happened. The precious treasure split, and cracked down the middle. Then a foul-smelling goo began to ooze out from inside.

'Crikey,' the other rats said. No one could understand it. Gold shouldn't behave like this.

But the Captain was trembling, for a terrible suspicion had stirred in his mind. Leaning over the broken brick, he drew his sword, and slashed off the wrapper.

'This isn't gold. It's chocolate,' he said.

CHAPTER TWELVE

For a few glorious moments, the Rats had believed they were rich. So the discovery that their gold was fake came as a savage blow.

'I'll skin those children alive!' roared the Captain. He was so cross the tip of his nose had turned purple.

He suspected that the mice had somehow been in on Arthur and Lucy's trick. He turned and glared at them, determined to make them pay.

'Do you still want to let them go?' the white rat asked stupidly.

'*Let them go?* Of course not, you fool! Do you think I intend to let them go after *this*? Pah! We shall take them back to the ship, and lock them in a cabin with no porthole, and keep them there for as long as they live on a diet of bread and water. Or maybe just water. That will teach them to try and make a fool out of me!'

Tumtum gulped. 'I say, Captain, we really didn't know anything about . . . I mean to say, we didn't—'

'Quiet!' the Captain snarled, baring a pair of yellow fangs. He turned to his Rats, and started giving orders. 'Load these filthy chocolates back into the margarine tub and cast them adrift. I want the children to find them, so they know we haven't fallen for their wicked ploy. If they want their mangy little mouse back, they'll have to come up with a better ransom than this.'

Tumtum and Nutmeg listened in horror. Events had taken a terrible turn.

'We must try and reason with him, dear,' Nutmeg trembled. And yet Captain Pong looked so cross that somehow they both felt tongue-tied.

The Nutmouses were so frightened, they did not notice the excited expression on General Marchmouse's face. So far, he had been behaving very feebly. But now he was looking at the chocolates very intently, and his brain had started to whirr.

'What sort of chocolates do you think these are, Mrs Nutmouse?' he whispered.

'They must be liqueurs,' Nutmeg said. 'Aunt Ivy gave Mr Mildew a box of them

131

132

at Christmas, and no one liked them, so they've been hanging around Rose Cottage ever since. The children must have dug them out of the larder, thinking they could play a trick on the Rats.'

'Liqueurs, eh?' the General said.

'That's right,' Nutmeg replied. 'You know the sort, General. Most humans have probably got some in their larder. They're dark and sickly, with revolting alcoholic drinks in the middle.'

The General's eyes gleamed. 'Yes, yes, I know what a liqueur is, Mrs Nutmouse,' he said impatiently. 'And if these are liqueurs, then we must persuade the Rats to eat them. We must ensure they eat *every single one.*'

'What good will that do?' asked Tumtum, who had been listening to this exchange.

'It will get them drunk!' the General hissed. 'And have you ever seen a drunk rat, Nutmouse?'

'I don't believe I have,' Tumtum replied. But the General was more worldly. He had seen many strange things during his army days.

'Well you've missed a thing or two, for

a drunk rat is a sight to behold,' he said knowingly.

'What are you getting at, General?' Tumtum asked, thinking this was no time for silly games. 'What's so special about a drunk rat?'

'I shall tell you what's special about a drunk rat, Nutmouse. A drunk rat can't chase after you. *That* is what's special about a drunk rat!'

The Nutmouses caught their breath, as what he was saying suddenly began to make sense. 'You mean to say—' Nutmeg began.

'I mean to say that if we can persuade the Rats to eat enough chocolates, then they'll fall down flat, and start wriggling their legs in the air, and hiccuping, and giggling, and—'

'And we can run away!' Nutmeg finished excitedly.

'Ah, but we won't run,' the General corrected her. 'We shall sail. As soon as the alcohol has taken its effect, the three of us will jump into the raft, and row out to *Lady Crossbones*. Then we'll climb on board, and pull up anchor, and sail away—leaving the Rats stranded on

134

Marchmouse Island!'

'What a heavenly plan,' Nutmeg said admiringly.

But Tumtum was foreseeing problems. 'Nutmeg and I tasted the chocolates once, and I can vouch that they're truly disgusting,' he said. 'Do you really think we could persuade the pirates to eat them?'

'Of course. Rats will eat anything,' the General replied confidently. But their conversation was suddenly cut short by Captain Pong.

'What are you muttering about?' he barked. 'Planning your escape, eh? Hah! You'll be lucky!'

The Rats had already finished loading the chocolates back into the margarine tub. And now they were dragging it to the water's edge. 'Cast her adrift!' Captain Pong shouted.

'I say, hang on!' the General cried.

The Rats glared at him. 'What do you want?' they snarled.

'Well, I suppose I don't want anything really,' the General replied, looking at the chocolate longingly. 'That's to say, well—I was just thinking what a shame it would be to let all this lovely treasure go to waste.'

'It isn't treasure. It's *chocolate*!' the Captain screeched. He was puce with fury. His disappointment was horrid enough as it was, without the General rubbing it in.

'But, my dear Captain, these aren't just any old chocolates,' the General persevered. 'They are Chocolate Liqueurs. Liqueurs, Captain. *Liqueurs!* Beautiful, rare, priceless things. Forget about gold, Captain. Oh, phooey! A whole boatful of gold is worth nothing compared to one Chocolate Liqueur.'

Captain Pong had not heard of chocolate liqueurs until now. So this was very puzzling to him. 'What's so special about them?' he asked.

The General feigned surprise. 'Gracious, Captain! What a sheltered life you've led. Why, liqueurs have magic centres. If you eat enough of them, anything becomes possible. I've known mice who would sell their own young for a single bite!'

The Rats had all gathered round, and were looking at the General suspiciously.

More intelligent rodents might have dismissed these wild claims straight away but the Rats did not know what to make of it. They had never been to school, and had not been taught to question things. Nonetheless, they were not completely taken in.

'Is there enough magic in them to make me rich?' Captain Pong asked greedily.

'Why, of course, my dear fellow!' the General exclaimed. 'Hah! You could become the richest rodent in the entire county, if you ate enough of them. Mr Nutmouse here owes his entire fortune to a chocolate liqueur, don't you, Nutty? One of his ancestors found one dropped under a Christmas tree, and—sensible mouse that he was—he bolted it down before anyone else could snatch it. And while he was eating, he made a wish. "I wish I had a grand house with a billiards room, and a ballroom, and a banqueting room, and a butler's room full of expensive china plates," he said. And next thing he knew, he owned Nutmouse Hall.'

'Is this true?' the Captain asked, turning to Tumtum.

'Quite true,' Tumtum replied.

Nutmeg caught her breath, for it was the first time she had heard him lie. Tumtum was surprised at himself too. But then he remembered that Captain Pong was threatening to lock them up in a dark cabin for the rest of their lives, on a diet of bread and water. And sometimes, when a threat such as that hangs over you, only a lie will do.

'My advice to you, Captain, would be to seize your chance, and scoff the whole lot,' Tumtum said. 'And remember, the more you eat, the richer you'll become,' he added encouragingly.

Captain Pong looked at Tumtum very carefully. Everyone knew that Mr Nutmouse was a learned mouse. It was rumoured he even had his own library. So perhaps his advice was worth taking. Besides, the thought of being rich made the Captain feel gloriously reckless.

'Pass me a chocolate,' he said.

CHAPTER THIRTEEN

There followed the most revolting scene. Tumtum had told the Rats that the more liqueurs they ate, the richer they would become. So they weren't going to let Captain Pong scoff the lot.

It was every rat for himself as they all fell upon the boat, tearing the gold wrappers off the chocolates, and frantically sinking their fangs into the dark shells. The chocolates were thick and hard, and the Rats had to gnaw like billy-o to reach the magic centres. As they finally chiselled through to the middle, each chocolate released a torrent of sickly syrup. Soon the whole beach was awash.

The Rats stood back in fright, for the liquid was giving off an overwhelming smell. It was like burned sugar, but much more intoxicating. It was so strong it made their eyes water.

'It's petrol,' one of them declared, holding his nose.

'It's poison,' another rat said.

140

Their suspicions were mounting. And the General's trick might easily have fallen through, had it not been for Tumtum's quick wittedness. He could see that the Rats needed encouragement— so he fell to his knees with a groan of delight and started slurping.

'Oh, heavenly nectar!' he cried, briefly coming up for air.

In actual fact, Tumtum was only pretending. He was not swallowing anything at all. But the Rats were fooled. And at the rate Tumtum appeared to be drinking, they feared there would be nothing left for them.

'Get out of there, you greedy brute!' Captain Pong grunted, hauling Tumtum aside by his collar.

Then all the Rats fell on the ground, and started spooning up huge pawfuls of the mysterious brown syrup. They ate with bitter rivalry. Not a word was exchanged. There was nothing to be heard but the smack, smack, smack of their jaws.

The mice watched anxiously, waiting for the first signs of silliness.

But the Rats just went on gorging.

141

Presently, however, Captain Pong rose to his knees, his face the colour of beetroot. He could sense a great giggle rising in his stomach. He was usually a very serious rat, but now he felt dizzy and carefree. It was as if all his ratty pride had been stripped away, and his head had been filled with treacle.

He turned to Tumtum, who looked a little fuzzy, and gave a loud hiccup. 'Good morrow to you, Mr Nutmouse,' he said. And of course it was a silly thing to say—but you'd say something silly too if you'd been gobbling chocolate liqueurs.

Without waiting for Tumtum to reply, the Captain staggered to the margarine tub, and pulled another chocolate from the pile.

Then the white rat lurched to his feet. He was also flushed, and there was syrup oozing down his chin. He made to follow Captain Pong. But he was walking very strangely. For every step he took forward, he went three steps back.

Finally he fell over and landed on his bottom.

The other Rats had got up now, and they were having a fine old time of it—stumbling about in the mud, and giggling until the tears coursed down their snouts. Then one of them grabbed another's paw, and soon they were all prancing in circles, braying their boating song to the moon.

Rob, rob, rob the boats,
Cruelly down the stream,
Greedily, greedily, greedily, greedily
Life is but a dream.

When they had finished, they all fell down.

Tumtum and Nutmeg looked on in astonishment. The General was right. A drunk rat was a sight to behold.

'Come on!' the General hissed. 'Now's our chance to escape.'

CHAPTER FOURTEEN

It was a glorious night to escape. The sky was a deep blue, and the moonlight was catching on the pond's surface, making it beam. The mice slunk silently across the beach and clambered into the raft. Then Tumtum and the General took the oars and started rowing out smoothly towards *Lady Crossbones*.

Nutmeg kept glancing back, fearing the Rats might suddenly pounce after them.

'I shouldn't worry if I were you,' the General said carelessly. 'They're in no state to chase us now. I tell you, they're so drunk, it will be morning before they even notice we're gone!'

They rowed around the ship's stern, and drew up on the far side, out of sight of the cove. The General tied the raft tightly to the guard rail, for they would need it when they had crossed The Pond. And with both the ship and the raft gone, the Rats would be stranded. They still had the margarine tub of course—but they would never be able to sail away in

146

that. It was barely big enough for one rat, let alone five.

When the raft was secure, the mice scrambled up the side of the ship and dropped down on to the deck. The lantern was still lit, casting a dull glow round the mast. There was a woodworm nibbling the water keg, and the remains of the Rats' supper—fly fillets and mashed slugs—had been left strewn on the stove.

Tumtum quickly began hauling up the anchor. But the General was too excited for such practicalities. Ever since he was a small boy, he had dreamed of having his own boat. And now he did. 'She's mine!' he cried, strutting the deck with delight.

'Steady on, General,' Tumtum said. 'We're only using her to escape in. You can't *keep* her. She's much too big for you.'

'Of course I can keep her,' the General replied. 'She shall become my private yacht. I shall repaint her, and replace that horrid cat with a handsome figurehead of myself. And I shall give her a new name, such as . . . well, such as *Lady*

148

Marchmouse. Yes, *Lady Marchmouse* has a pleasant ring to it.'

'But what will you do with her?' Tumtum asked. He was tugging down on the sails, anxious to be off. 'A yacht is a big responsibiliy you know.'

'Oh, fiddlesticks,' replied the General, who seemed in no hurry to set sail. 'I shall moor her along the stream—somewhere nice and tucked away, where the stoats and the otters won't find her. And then, whenever there's a nice sunny day, I shall come rap-tap-tapping at your door, Mr Nutmouse, saying, "Do join me for a cruise on the *Lady Marchmouse*," that's what I'll say. Then we shall wave our wives toodle-pip, and off we'll go on our pleasure boat—just you and me, titans of the stream, waving royally to all we see!'

Neither Tumtum nor Nutmeg liked the sound of this. But their bigger concern was getting home. 'Come on, General. Help me tighten the sails,' Tumtum said.

Neither mouse was an experienced sailor, so much of what followed was guesswork. They heaved down on various ropes, and pulled on this lever and that—until suddenly they felt a great force above them. The mast heaved. The cloth strained. Then the grey sails flared out in the breeze.

The General ran to the wheel and wrenched it down, until the ship was pointing away from the island. They were free at last, slicing silently towards the moonlit horizon. And they might easily have escaped unseen, for the Rats had not noticed the ship pulling away. But the General could not resist a chance to show off.

'Take the wheel,' he ordered Tumtum; then he grabbed the lantern down from the mast, and raced back to the stern. The ship was inching on fast, but he could still see the Rats dancing on the shore. He leaned over the rail, filled his lungs with air, and shouted, 'Cheerio!'

The Rats heard the General's voice echoing around the cove. They wobbled to a halt and looked stupidly over their shoulders. Then they turned towards The Pond, and finally noticed their ship blowing away.

'Oi,' they all cried. They stumbled to the shore and waded drunkenly into the

water, their joy giving way to a terrible rage.

'Come back or we'll eat you alive!' Captain Pong roared. But his threats were empty now, and *Lady Crossbones* sailed on heedlessly into the night. Soon all the Rats could see was the silhouette of the great General Marchmouse, waving gloatingly from the stern.

*   *   *

'We're free!' Nutmeg said rapturously, grasping Tumtum's paw. And even Tumtum let out a whoop, so relieved was he to have escaped.

But their trials were not over yet. For the voyage was long and gruelling, and *Lady Crossbones* proved devilishly hard to control.

No sooner had she blown two metres from the shore, than she was caught by a fierce headwind, which sent her buffeting round in circles.

Tumtum and Nutmeg tugged with all their might on the sail, and the General tried to wrench the wheel, but the gusts were too strong for them, and *Lady*

Crossbones refused to go on.

'Blast this vessel,' the General fumed. 'What's the use of a ship that dances round in circles?' He had already burned his paws pulling on the sail ropes, and he was in a foul humour. Being in command of such a big ship wasn't turning out to be nearly such fun as he'd expected. He wished he had a smaller, nimbler boat— like *Bluebottle*. But *Bluebottle* was no more.

Eventually, the swell eased, and the breeze caught in the sails again, nudging them on. But when they had gone a little further, a freak wave smashed over the deck, tipping the boat to starboard, and nearly washing Nutmeg overboard.

'Aah!' she cried, clinging for dear life to the mast. Tumtum and the General both rushed to her side and held her tight. When the ship steadied they all collapsed on the deck, soaked through and exhausted.

It was a miserable voyage. And to make matters worse, there was no fresh water, and nothing to eat but the rancid remains of the Rats' supper. And there weren't even any comfortable beds.

*　　*　　*

It was many hours later, and almost light, when *Lady Crossbones* finally approached the main bank of The Pond. 'Land Ahoy!' the General cried weakly, guiding her in round a clump of rushes.

By the time the ship reached dry land, even General Marchmouse was fed up. 'I'm not sure *Lady Crossbones* is the right boat for me,' he said.

'Hmmm. What did I tell you?' Tumtum replied. 'Well, never mind, General. If you don't want her we can just abandon her here on the bank.'

'We can't do that,' the General said. 'If we leave her here the Rats will reclaim her—they're sure to find their way back from the island one day. And once they've got *Lady Crossbones* back, they'll be able to start pirating again.'

Tumtum considered this a moment. The General was right—without their ship the Rats would be much less dangerous.

'I've an idea,' Nutmeg said. 'Why don't we give *Lady Crossbones* to the children, as a present? It was our fault that *Bluebottle* sank, so now we can make it up to them. I can leave them a letter in the attic tonight, explaining what's happened, and telling them that if they come down to The Pond as soon as they've had breakfast, they'll find a new boat waiting for them. Imagine how delighted they'll be!'

'That's a splendid plan,' Tumtum said.

'We can warn them that she'll need a good scrub,' Nutmeg went on. 'And I'll tell them to repaint her, and give her a new name, so everyone will know she's not a pirate ship any more.'

'Well that's settled then,' the General said, relieved to have the ship off his paws.

*   *   *

As the three mice lowered the sails, ready to disembark, the General looked back a moment at The Pond, searching through the weeds and the rushes for one last glimpse of Marchmouse Island. But it was invisible now, lost beyond the vast horizon. He felt a stab of longing. It was *his* island, his alone; and one of these days he would go back there. But The Pond looked so big, he wondered if he would ever find it again.

He turned back to the shore, and saw the dawn rising beyond the meadow. With a sudden start, he realised that he had been away from the gun cupboard for three whole nights. He had given Mrs Marchmouse clear instructions not to worry about him—but he suspected she might not be following them.

'I had better be getting home,' he said.

CHAPTER FIFTEEN

A few hours later, Lucy woke up. She wanted to find out if Nutmeg had come back. But suddenly she felt afraid. Instead of rushing out of bed she turned her face into the pillow and lay with her eyes tight shut.

A minute went by, then she shook herself together and sat up. Arthur was still sleeping. Quietly, so as not to wake him, she walked over to the chest of drawers. And with a rush of relief, she saw a tiny envelope propped against her hairbrush.

'Arthur, she's back!' she cried. While her brother was still rubbing his eyes, she found the magnifying glass in the drawer of her bedside table, and read Nutmeg's letter out loud.

Dear Arthur and Lucy,
Thanks to your wonderful trick I have escaped. But events took quite a turn, and went much better than we might have planned. In the end, I stole

Lady Crossbones *from under the Rats' very snouts, and sailed her home by the light of the moon, leaving the pirates marooned on the island. It was quite a night!*

But we must never allow the pirates to reclaim their ship—for then they would start pirating again. So from now on, Lady Crossbones *belongs to you. She will need a wash, of course, and a fresh coat of paint, and perhaps a dab of superglue on her rudder. But for the most part she is in good shape, and I believe you will find much to admire in her. I have moored her on the southern bank of The Pond, near the tree stump with moss on it.*

Now hurry, my dears, and claim her before someone else does.
Love,
Nutmeg.

P.S. I would not send the Rats any more chocolates if I were you. Rich food has a bad effect on them.

The children were overwhelmed. At best they had hoped they would get Nutmeg back. They hadn't expected a new boat as well.

'Come on, let's go and find it,' Arthur said.

They got dressed then hurried downstairs and let themselves out into the garden. It was very early. The village had not yet stirred, and the grass was still covered in dew. They shut the back door quietly, so as not to wake their father, then ran across the meadow to The Pond.

The children did not know which way was south, but they soon spotted the tree stump that Nutmeg had described. It was on the far side of The Pond, where the grass had been trampled by sheep. They ran over to it, and when they parted the rushes they found *Lady Crossbones*, moored against the bank.

She did not look so menacing at close range. Her huge grey sails had been tied down, and there was a snail snoozing on the deck. The children carefully lifted the boat from the water, and stood it on the grass. Then they knelt down and peered through the portholes, examining each cabin in turn.

Everything looked very real. There were rugs on the floor, and blankets on the beds, and clothes spewing from the chests of drawers. And there were paintings hanging from the walls—big gloomy portraits, mainly of rats—and silver candlesticks on the bedside tables.

Arthur felt no regrets for *Bluebottle* now. This was the best toy boat he had ever seen.

'Nutmeg's right, we should repaint her. Black's too sinister,' Lucy said. 'And we should give her a new name. *Lady Crossbones* sounds silly.'

'Let's call her *Lady Nutmeg*,' Arthur said. Lucy agreed to this. So *Lady Nutmeg* she became.

'Do you think the pirates will be stuck on the island for ever?' Lucy said.

Arthur shrugged. 'I don't see how they'll get back without a boat.'

It was strange to think there were pirates on The Pond. But many strange things had happened to Arthur and Lucy recently, so they supposed it must be true. They longed for a glimpse of them—but when they looked across to the island all they could see was the margarine tub upturned on the bank, and a few gold chocolate wrappers scattered along the shore.

'I wonder if we'll ever see them,' Lucy said.

'I should think we're bound to one day,' Arthur replied. Though he wasn't sure he wanted to. He'd had enough of pirates for now. 'Come on. Let's take *Lady Nutmeg* home and start painting her,' he said.

They lifted the boat between them, for it was very heavy, and turned back towards the cottage. But had they watched the island a moment longer, they would have seen something stir. For just then Captain Pong, who had slept all night under a chocolate wrapper in the cove, rolled over and gave a loud belch.

*   *   *

Meanwhile, the General had returned home to a tearful reception from Mrs Marchmouse. Just as he feared, she had been worrying about him without stop. The General often went off exploring on his own, but it was most unlike him to stay away for as long as this.

She was beginning to feel sure something awful must have happened to him. And she was just putting on her bonnet, ready to go out and summon help, when suddenly he burst through the gun cupboard door.

'Marchie!' she cried weakly, throwing herself upon his mousely chest; and the General was so touched by her concern that he promised he would never go adventuring again.

This would have come as welcome news to Tumtum and Nutmeg, who felt the General had embroiled them in quite enough trouble as it was. The last few days had been a terrible ordeal, and it was a wonderful moment when they finally crept back into the broom cupboard, and saw their beloved Nutmouse Hall again.

They had been away so long that everything looked dusty and neglected. A fly had knocked over the milk jug on the kitchen table, and there was a spider bathing in the sink.

Nutmeg was too tired to tackle these

164

upsets now. She had barely slept all night, and she could feel herself fading. Tumtum suddenly noticed how drawn she looked. 'You sit down and I'll make some breakfast,' he said.

They both felt much better when they had eaten some porridge. Then Tumtum made a pot of tea, and they sat at the table for a long while, mulling things over.

'What is the matter with us, Tumtum?' Nutmeg asked. 'No sooner is one adventure over, than another seems to come along.'

Tumtum leaned back in his chair, considering this problem. What they both liked most of all was peace and quiet, so all this excitement did seem rather bad luck. But then it occurred to him they might not appreciate their peaceful days nearly so much if there wasn't the occasional adventure to interrupt them.

And he was about to explain this to Nutmeg, but he dozed off while thinking how to phrase it.

*　　*　　*

As for the Rats, there is not much more to say about them. The Captain had become quite frenzied when he saw the mice escaping in his ship, and had tried to chase after them in the margarine tub. But it was much too small for him, and he was rather drunk—so he had capsized a few inches from the shore.

The other Rats could say nothing to console him that evening. But next morning, when they all took stock of the situation, things didn't seem so bad. For it was a glorious day, and they still had lots of chocolates left. And now that General Marchmouse had gone, the island was all theirs again. Which made them feel quite rich in a way—for as Captain Pong rightly observed, it's not every rat who has an island in the sun.

166